MURDER AT THE SAVOY

A GINGER GOLD MYSTERY BOOK 18

LEE STRAUSS

Library and Archives Canada Cataloguing in Publication

Title: Murder at the Savoy / Lee Strauss.

Names: Strauss, Lee (Novelist), author.

Series: Strauss, Lee (Novelist). Ginger Gold mystery ; 18.

Description: Series statement: A Ginger Gold mystery ; 18 | "A 1920s cozy historical mystery." Identifiers: Canadiana (print) 2021033262X | Canadiana (ebook) 20210332638 | ISBN 9781774091968 (hardcover) | ISBN 9781774091944 (softcover) | ISBN 9781774091951 (IngramSpark softcover) | ISBN 9781774091975 (Kindle) | ISBN 9781774091982 (EPUB) Classification: LCC PS8637.T739 M8745 2022 | DDC C813/.6—dc23

GINGER GOLD MYSTERIES

(IN ORDER)

Murder on the SS *Rosa*

Murder at Hartigan House

Murder at Bray Manor

Murder at Feathers & Flair

Murder at the Mortuary

Murder at Kensington Gardens

Murder at St. George's Church

The Wedding of Ginger & Basil

Murder Aboard the Flying Scotsman

Murder at the Boat Club

Murder on Eaton Square

Murder by Plum Pudding

Murder on Fleet Street

Murder at Brighton Beach

Murder in Hyde Park

Murder at the Royal Albert Hall

Murder in Belgravia

Murder on Mallowan Court

Murder at the Savoy

Murder at the Circus

Murder at the Boxing Club

Kensington Addison Road train station was a beehive of excited, anxious, and weary travellers: hurrying or waiting, hugging loved ones, or sauntering off alone. Some collapsed damp umbrellas as others waited in the queue to make a purchase at the tea and sandwich stall. Steam trains chugged and whistled, spewing black smoke, as they either slowed to a stop or wound up to speed away.

Mrs. Ginger Reed, known by some as Lady Gold, stood at the barrier at the end of the platform with her husband, Basil, a man she adored and whose good looks —warm hazel eyes, greying temples, and a debonair stance—garnered the admiration of many female pedestrians as they passed by. Like Ginger, some of the women dressed in the latest spring of 1927 fashions: pleated skirts landing just below the knee, fitted spring jackets with long collars and hems hitting the lower hips, colourful scarves or masculine-like ties adorning the neck, and the quintessential cloche hat covering short-cropped hair.

Ginger, too, was used to getting similar glances of appreciation from the opposite sex—her red locks often caught the eye—but the baby in her arms kept looks from lingering.

Ginger was more than fine with the exchange. She had her man and her baby. Smiling down at her dark-haired little girl, she said, "Rosa, love, you're about to meet your Aunt Louisa and Grandma Sally!"

"Do you see them?" Basil asked as a new group of passengers disembarked from the Liverpool train.

Ginger craned her neck, looking for the familiar faces, Louisa with dark hair and familiar green eyes, Sally with salt-and-pepper locks. Ginger's emotions were a mix of anticipation and apprehension. She loved her half-sister dearly and harboured a measure of fondness for her stepmother, but rarely was time spent with either of them a relaxing event. Her American relatives seemed to love drama and brought it wherever they went.

Suddenly, there they were. Ginger handed Rosa to Abby Green, their competent, sturdy-looking nanny who'd been hanging back, and then lifted her arm into the air. "Louisa! Sally!"

Louisa grabbed her mother's arm as they hurried over. A gentleman wearing a brown fedora followed behind, but Ginger assumed he was a fellow passenger headed in the same direction.

"Ginger!" Louisa squealed as she threw an arm around Ginger's shoulder. She then fell into Basil's arms, startling him. Ginger missed this enthusiastic affection. The British were much more reserved. A similar round of hugs, if less affectionate, continued with Sally, which immediately moved to American-accented baby-talk as Nanny Green held Rosa out for inspection.

"Oh, Ginger," Louisa said. "She's a doll!"

Sally sent Ginger a look of approval. "Well done."

Ginger laughed. "I can hardly take full credit but thank you."

The gentleman in the fedora hovered behind, a broad grin on his face, and Ginger raised a brow in question.

Louisa took the fellow's arm, her face breaking into a wide smile. "Ginger, Basil, this is Cornelius Gastrell, my fiancé!"

Ginger, a master at keeping her emotions reined in, allowed herself to express her surprise. "Louisa?"

"I know, I know. I wanted it to be a surprise!"

"And it is," Ginger said. She offered a hand to Louisa's gentleman. "Mr. Gastrell, it's a pleasure."

"The pleasure's mine, ma'am," he said with a drawl. "And you must call me Cornelius."

Cornelius moved to shake Basil's hand. "Good to meet you, Basil," he said, probably assuming they were all on a first-name basis. He whistled. "Never been to London before. Can't wait to see what all the fuss is about."

"Shall we head to the motorcars?" Basil asked. They'd brought Ginger's Crossley and Basil's Austin to accommodate everyone.

Cornelius walked ahead with Basil as the ladies followed behind.

Louisa gripped Ginger's arm. "Isn't he just the bee's knees, Ginger?" Her words burst forth like a fountain with the water pressure too high. "Can you believe I'm to be married? Finally! You must come back to Boston for the wedding."

Sally laid a hand on her daughter's shoulder and added with less enthusiasm. "A date hasn't been set yet. Now, let Ginger catch her breath."

Mr. Gastrell drove back with Basil whilst Louisa and Sally went with Ginger. There was much to catch up on during the drive back to Hartigan House, and Ginger shared about life with Rosa, presently held tightly by Nanny Green, and Scout, who was away at boarding school. Louisa boasted about the social scene in Boston, which Ginger found entertaining but didn't miss.

Mrs. Beasley, Ginger's cook, had luncheon prepared for when they got back, and once everyone was settled in their rooms at Hartigan House, they descended on the dining room. Added to their number around the long wooden table was the Dowager Lady Gold, the grandmother of Ginger's late husband, Daniel, Lord Gold, and Daniel's sister, Felicia, and her new husband, Charles Davenport-Witt, the Earl of Witt.

Introductions were made and places taken. Once the maids had served the roast duck and potatoes, conversation resumed. The electric chandelier overhead created a pleasant ambience, highlighting the paintings hung from a picture rail along the top of the walls.

"Nice pad you have here," Cornelius said. "Everything around here seems as old as the hills."

Ginger wasn't certain if she should say thank you or not. "Hartigan House has been in the family for ages. It's my childhood home. I inherited it from my father when he passed away."

"And I got the crummy brownstone," Louisa said with a pout.

"It's hardly *crummy*," Sally said sternly. "It's in a

coveted Boston neighbourhood." She gave everyone at the table a look, then added, "On the Commons."

Louisa had the decency to look sheepish. "I know, Mama. I was only teasing."

An awkward silence filled the room, broken, thankfully, by Basil. "Did anyone catch the Boat Race yesterday?"

"We listened to it on the wireless on the BBC," Felicia said. Like Louisa, she had dark hair cut in a bob, though hers had been ironed into waves. "It's the first time it's been broadcast that way."

"If I were a betting man," Charles started, "I would've called Oxford, but Cambridge won by three lengths."

"It's a shame we missed it," Ginger said. "Basil's work called him away, and I was busy with the baby."

Cornelius, becoming less charming by the moment, held a fist to his mouth, barely concealing a small belch. "What kind of boats are we talking about here?"

"Rowing boats," Basil said. "The Boat Race is always between Oxford and Cambridge." For clarity, he added, "Universities."

"Row boats?" Cornelius huffed. "Not motorboats? Y'all have a different idea of a worthwhile sporting event."

Basil stiffened. "I'm not sure what—"

"Take that game y'all like over here where they try to combine baseball with bowling or some such thing."

Ambrosia blinked slowly, her round eyes looking more bulbous. "Do you mean *cricket*, Mr. Gastrell?"

"That's it!" Cornelius slapped a thigh. "Named after a bug! Now baseball, that's a man's game."

"You do realise cricket has been around for hundreds of years longer than baseball," Basil said.

Cornelius grinned. "Old doesn't make it better."

"I've heard about the baseball ball player who recently signed a contract for an absurd amount of money." Charles said.

"Seventy thousand smackers!" Cornelius said as if it were he who'd come into the fortune and not a sports celebrity.

"Seventy thousand American dollars?" Felicia asked. "Is that a lot?

"It's around fifty thousand pounds," Charles answered.

Felica gaped. "To play a game?"

"Americans have their priorities," Basil said dryly.

"Darn tootin' they do," Cornelius replied. "We work hard and play hard."

Ginger forced a blank expression. She glanced at her sister, who'd become uncharacteristically quiet.

"Have you nothing to offer on the subject?"

"No," Louisa said firmly. "Sports bore me."

Basil wasn't so keen to let the man's comment ride. "So, Mr. Gastrell, what do you do for work in America?"

"Watch the stock market." Cornelius stabbed a piece of duck flesh with his fork, waving it about as he continued. "You will, too, if you're smart. Easiest money I've ever made."

When the table was cleared of lunch, Lizzie, one of the family maids and Ginger's favourite, brought the tea tray.

"Thank you, Lizzie," Ginger said.

The diminutive maid nodded her pointy chin then bobbed before leaving again.

"What about coffee?" Cornelius shouted after her. He laughed at the table of stunned faces. "Can't stand that dishwater you call tea."

Lizzie raced back into the dining room, her wide eyes on Ginger. "Madam?"

"Ask Mrs. Beasley to brew a pot of coffee for our guest."

"Yes, madam."

Cornelius went on. "You sure do know how to train your help around here." He draped an arm around Louisa. "Maybe we should ship a couple of maids over to Boston. It can be my wedding present to you."

Ambrosia sat straight and stiff thanks to an antiquated corset. She looked regal with her jewelled hands and flowing day frock as she let out a breath of disbelief. "Dear me, how one talks in America."

"We like to get to the point," Sally returned. "When George was alive, God rest his soul, it used to make me crazy how he circled to get to what he was driving at."

"A measure of propriety and self-control benefits society," Ambrosia offered.

"Americans have self-control," Louisa said defensively. "We just say what we mean."

Ambrosia's lips—deeply lined and uncoloured—twitched. "How delightful for you."

Ginger loudly cleared her throat, then turned to Felicia, desperate to change the subject. "Have you decided on wallpaper?" To her new guests, she explained, "Felicia and Charles have recently acquired and moved into the house across the street."

Charles had a larger family home in London, but Felicia, new to the role of mistress of her own residence, had found the prospect overwhelming, especially since her new husband's work often took him away from home.

Ginger was happy to have Felicia nearby on Mallowan Court. Felicia had lived at Hartigan House before she married, and Ginger had missed her terribly when she'd moved out. As a bonus, she could help her former sister-in-law decorate!

"I'm going to go with the paisley print for the living room and lilies for the drawing room," Felicia said. "At least I think so."

"Excellent choices," Ginger said. "I shall bring Rosa over later to have a look." Then, to be polite, she addressed her guests. "What are the plans for you three?"

"We'll take the rest of the day to rest," Louisa said, "but tomorrow we have plans for the opera; first we're going to stroll around the grounds of Buckingham Palace." She patted Cornelius' arm. "Cornie's hoping to get a glimpse of the King."

"I'm afraid the public aren't allowed on the grounds," Ginger said, "but you will be able to watch the Change of the Guard at the front of the palace."

"I'm eager to see this New Scotland Yard," Cornelius said, his eyebrows lifting.

"Oh, yes," Basil began. "I'm afraid the Yard is not meant for tourists. You're welcome to walk along the Victoria Embankment, however. The architecture of the building is delightful."

Cornelius guffawed. "*Delightful.* If American men used words like that, we'd be lynched on the street."

Even Ginger couldn't keep a gasp from escaping her lips.

"Really, Cornelius," Sally said, her jaw tight. "Some sentiments are worth keeping to yourself."

Having never bonded with her stepmother, Ginger felt a rare sense of appreciation for the woman who was proving to be more sensible than Ginger had remembered.

Then, as if on cue, Ginger's faithful butler, Pippins, tall with shoulders folding forward from seventy years of effort, entered, his blue eyes flashing. He carried a silver tray that held a single envelope.

Approaching Basil, he said, "The afternoon post, sir." With a barely perceptible glance at the American contingent at the table, he added, "I thought you'd like it now."

"Oh yes," Basil said, obviously eager for a diversion. He picked up the envelope and stared at the handwriting of his name on the front.

"Do you recognise it?" Ginger asked. She wondered if Basil would excuse himself and leave them all in suspense, but he removed the folded piece of paper.

"Darling?" Ginger said.

"It's from an old acquaintance, a Percy Aspen. He's been out of the country for eleven years and has just returned. He's asking us to join him for dinner tomorrow night at the Savoy." His warm hazel eyes landed on Ginger. "He says to bring my new family."

To Ginger, this would include Felicia and Charles, and Ambrosia. However, at present, her family went beyond that, and Louisa burst out joyously. "The Savoy! That sounds scrummy. Cornelius, we must go to the Savoy."

"What's so great about the Savoy?" Cornelius asked, giving Ginger a moment of hope that he'd veto the idea.

"It's a hotel. The most luxurious, and a favourite of the rich and famous," Louisa said. "Almost as much as the Ritz."

"And a breakthrough in modern engineering," Charles added. "Electricity is steam generated with water provided by the hotel's own artesian wells. One can turn the room lights on and off at will, and hot water is available whenever needed."

"The hotel also has a grisly past," Felicia added with a glint in her eye. "Four years ago, a wealthy young Egyptian prince was murdered by his French wife."

"Sounds like an unhappy union," Sally said with a half glance at her daughter.

"Indeed," Ginger said. "The widow was acquitted when it was revealed that her husband had treated her cruelly and had threatened to kill her." Ginger hoped the morbid story would divert her sister's interest. To Louisa, she said, "What about the opera? Are you sure you want to miss that?"

"We can go to that another day," Louisa said,

squelching Ginger's hopes. Louisa turned to Sally. "Right, Mama?"

"I don't know," Sally said. "This Percy fellow won't be expecting us."

"He said for Basil to bring his new family," Louisa protested. She motioned dramatically to herself, Sally, and Cornelius. "That's us!"

Ginger flashed an apologetic look at Basil and whispered, "Perhaps we should tell him we will meet him another time."

"Aspen is quite clear it has to be tomorrow night. He's leaving the next morning on important business."

Ginger did a quick headcount. "Felicia and Charles?"

Charles chuckled. "Wouldn't miss it."

Relieved, Ginger went on to Ambrosia. "Grandmother, you shall join us?"

It was a directive disguised as a question. She needed the elderly lady there to keep Sally company and to help smooth out the conversation.

"I suppose I shall," Ambrosia said with a twist of her lips. "I fear I owe you a favour or two."

"Fabulous." Ginger reached for Basil's hand. "Do tell Mr. Aspen we'll be pleased to join him. Our number is eight."

2

The next morning was pleasant and *peaceful* —her energetic guests having gone sight-seeing. The strength of Ginger's love for her daughter, with her round green eyes and tiny bow-shaped lips, amazed her. She admitted to brief disappointment when it became clear that her baby wasn't a redhead as she herself was, but Rosa's eyes definitely came from her mother.

Almost five months old, little Rosa was learning to sit on her own, enjoying success for several minutes before toppling over like a pile of laundry into the pillows Ginger had propped up around her on her four-poster bed. Ginger laughed as she propped Rosa back up. "You're doing so well, little one. Soon you'll be crawling and getting into things, so I'm just going to enjoy this time whilst I have a measure of control."

A soft tap on the door was followed by the entrance of Rosa's nurse. Abby Green had been a godsend. Older than Ginger, the nanny had a strong constitution, both intellectually and physically.

"Would you like me to take her, madam?" Nanny said. "She'll be ready for a nappy change soon." She tapped her watch. "You wanted extra time to get ready for this evening's activities?"

"Yes, thank you, Nanny," Ginger said as she lifted Rosa up, kissed her on the cheek with much enthusiasm, and handed her over.

Though Ginger did indeed want extra time to prepare for dinner at the Savoy, she also wanted a little peace and quiet to write a letter to Scout before Basil returned from work. She feared her adopted son might harbour resentment at being sent to Kingswell Academy, even though she and Basil had reassured him it was a normal thing for a boy in his circumstances to do. Unfortunately, the timing had matched Rosa's arrival, and Ginger didn't want Scout to associate the new baby with his departure. She committed to writing to him every other day to ensure he knew he was loved and thought of often.

Taking the curved staircase, Ginger moved down the emerald-green carpet runner to the polished black-and-white tile entrance hall. A large chandelier with newly installed electric lights hung from the upper-story ceiling, providing a fairy-tale glow. She passed the tall wooden doors of the sitting room and headed down a corridor that led to her office. From the opened baize door into the kitchen, she glimpsed Mrs. Beasley, a round-looking woman with a full skirt, a white apron, and greying curls topped with a white cook's mob-cap. She and her helpers in the kitchen were taking the opportunity of a night off from providing dinner to bake for the coming days and catch up on cleaning.

After Ginger had inherited Hartigan House, she'd decided she wouldn't return to Boston. Once again, she would make London her home. She was set on doing a top-to-bottom redecoration. Every room was redesigned and refitted except for this one: her father's study. Ginger had kept it much the way it always had been, with her father's business books on the shelves, the walls painted a dark maroon, and heavy dark-wood furnishing and trim. His desk faced a stone fireplace, which a maid had kept lit, and a bed for Boss, currently occupied, lay nearby.

"Hey, Bossy, there you are."

Her dog had become rather attached to Scout and seemed to suffer from the lack of near-constant attention the lad had given him. He was good with Rosa but didn't appear to like sharing.

Ginger scooped him into her arms and nuzzled his face. "We all have to adapt to change, Bossy, even you."

Settling into her office chair with Boss on her lap, Ginger removed a sheet of paper from her drawer, picked up a fountain pen—her favourite with a gold-plated nib—and wrote. "Dearest Scout . . ." She fell into a rhythm as she related the antics of Aunt Louisa and Mrs. Hartigan and Aunt Louisa's friend, along with a few anecdotes about Rosa. Ginger hoped Scout would grow fond of his sister over time.

"What would you like to say, Boss?" Ginger imagined her dog's conversation, greeting Scout in what she hoped sounded like a puppy voice, and imagining her son's smile as he read it.

"What have we here?"

Ginger's head bobbed up towards the voice of her husband. "Boss and I are writing to Scout."

"Jolly good. Do send my greetings."

"Of course." Ginger included *cheers from Dad*, embellishing a little by adding that he was looking forward to a game of tennis when Scout returned home.

After including her own salutations of love, Ginger folded the letter, put it in an envelope, and delivered it to Lizzie to drop into the nearest postbox.

Boss followed her upstairs, his nails clicking on the tiles like they'd done countless times before, returning to her bedroom.

Designed with sophistication, the room contained a

large four-poster bed, chest of drawers, wardrobe, dressing table, and standing mirror, all made from matching, elaborately designed rosewood. The quilt and pillows had a gold-and-ivory print that complemented the gold-and-ivory-striped chairs hugging a round table in front of the long windows.

Basil entered after her, still damp from the bathroom at the end of the corridor. His dark hair was slicked back, and he smelled delightfully of lemon-scented soap. She couldn't resist pulling him into her arms, his hazel eyes crinkling at the corners as he grinned back in surprise.

"Mrs. Reed! I'm in my dressing gown. This could delay our departure and make us late."

Ginger kissed her husband then pushed him away.

"That would never do. I'm entirely curious to meet this old friend of yours, Mr. Percy Aspen." She cocked her head. "You've never spoken of him."

"I wouldn't classify him as a friend, per se," Basil said. "More of an acquaintance, rather. Someone I met during an old case."

Ginger opened her wardrobe, eyeing the different frocks that hung there. "What type of man is he? Perhaps your answer might give me a clue as to which frock to wear."

"I'd rather you'd dress for me, love, than him."

Ginger pulled out an off-the-shoulder, turquoise

dinner gown that had a splash of sequins from the waist down, increasing in density as it fell to the handkerchief hemline. Holding it up to her torso, she asked, "How about this?"

"Simply divine."

Draping the gown over a chair, she waited for Basil to finish buttoning his starched white shirt before helping with his black bow tie. "You never answered my question."

"About?"

Ginger sensed her husband's reluctance to talk about his old acquaintance, which only piqued her curiosity further. "Mr. Aspen. Basil?" she added with a chiding tone. "You're being so secretive."

Basil strolled to one of the gold-and-white-striped armchairs that nestled at the table.

"There's not that much to say, love," he said. "I'm rather perplexed, truth be told. I haven't seen him in years. I'm more curious than anything."

Normally, Ginger would ring for Lizzie to help her dress, but she didn't want to give Basil an excuse to leave before answering her questions. She unbuttoned her frock, revealing a full-length silk slip. "Then why the sudden need to meet you and your *new* family?" she asked. "And dinner at the Savoy? Not your run-of-the-mill eatery."

"Aspen has spent the last eleven or so years travelling with an archaeologist, digging up bones and arte-facts and the like in Africa and South America. Whilst in Africa, he apparently struck it rich, investing in a gold mine. Or was it diamonds? Either way, he's a much richer bloke now than the Aspen I knew."

Ginger sat at her dressing table and regarded her reflection. Fine lines had formed around her green eyes, with more threatening her forehead. She'd had Lizzie pluck a grey hair just the week before! She'd turn thirty-four in the summer, and there wasn't much she could do about her age. Her thin brows arched high over her lids and needed cleaning up. As she picked up her tweezers and plucked, she caught Basil's gaze in the mirror.

"His reaching out to you out of the blue is rather peculiar, is it not?" she said. "And how did you and Mr. Aspen meet again? Did you go to university together?" She cocked her head. "The Great War?"

Basil had been invalided out in the first year, a trauma that had charted his course to Scotland Yard, where he meant to do his "bit". He stayed on after-wards, not because of the money, of which he had plenty, but because he realised he was good at the work and found personal fulfilment in solving crimes and putting criminals away.

"No, not the war," Basil said after a beat. "But shortly after I started at the Yard. It was my first case as an inspector and rather dramatic. I served under Morris, who was a chief inspector at the time."

Ginger wrinkled her nose at the mention of Superintendent Morris, an arrogant man whom she barely tolerated.

Basil continued. "We brought down a reigning kingpin in London's gangster underworld."

"Really?" Ginger replaced her tweezers with a brown eyebrow pencil. The trouble being a redhead was that one's eyebrows seemed to disappear, especially in the dim light found in the dining room at the Savoy. "I don't remember you mentioning this dramatic case."

"I suppose it's because it wasn't really mine, though I did end up testifying."

Ginger straightened. "To put a gangster in prison?"

Basil flicked a hand and crossed his legs. "It was a long time ago."

"Eleven years."

Basil shrugged. "There have been so many cases since then, I've hardly thought about it."

Ginger brushed her bob, pinning it with gem-encrusted barrettes off her forehead. "And how does Mr. Aspen fit in?"

"He was also a witness, though, unlike my testimony, his was the death knell. Aspen's not the bravest sort, especially when the potential of violence is involved, perhaps because he has terrible eyesight—which is why he wasn't in the trenches. Before I knew it, he'd left the country."

Ginger darkened her eyelids with powder and finished her make-up by applying dark red lipstick. She smacked her lips together then turned to face Basil. "What did Mr. Aspen see?"

"The books. He was a new employee of an accountancy firm, and apparently, the only one who hadn't yet been bought off." Basil tugged on his trousers as he got to his feet. He leaned to kiss Ginger on the cheek, then said, "I'm going to say goodnight to Rosa. I'll meet you downstairs."

Ginger watched Basil go, then rang for Lizzie; she needed Lizzie's help with the buttons of her gown. As she waited, she found her mind was on this mysterious Percy Aspen. She really couldn't wait to meet him.

3

*B*asil and Ginger walked together through one of the two revolving doors that served as an entrance to the Savoy hotel in the heart of London. They both stopped for a moment, standing hand in hand, to take in the ornate surroundings. The place was grand by anyone's definition, and Basil had to admire the black-and-white-marble floor, polished high ceiling, and endless gold ornamentation. Massive square columns, painted white, dominated the room, whilst a long oakwood reception desk took up the far end.

Close behind them were Charles and Felicia, along with Ambrosia assisted by her silver-handled walking stick.

"I simply adore the Savoy," Felicia said. "It really is

a marvel. Just look at all the electric lighting. It's magical."

Ambrosia concurred. "Indeed. It's some sort of sorcery."

"As I said yesterday, the hotel's electricity is generated using steam from the hotel's artesian wells," Charles added. "All the other luxury hotels are blushing with shameful inadequacy."

A moment later, they were joined by Sally and Louisa, the latter arm in arm with the odious Cornelius Gastrell. Basil resisted the urge to pinch his nostrils in protest. When one married, one was bestowed with the beloved's family. Basil could take comfort in the fact that Ginger's future brother-in-law would eventually be returning to America with Louisa and Sally.

"Well, this place sure is ritzy," Louisa said.

Gastrell whistled loudly. "I feel the need to bow to someone." Facing Louisa and Sally, he bent at the waist and, with a terrible English accent, said, "My lady, my lady."

Louisa laughed aloud. "Oh, Cornie!"

Basil didn't miss Ambrosia's bulbous eyes bulging further with mortification. Hastening to rein everyone together, he cleared his throat. "Shall we?"

"Lead on, man," Gastrell said.

"Of course," Basil returned cordially. "According to the invitation, we will be dining in the Pinafore Room."

He turned to the concierge. "We're with Percy Aspen's party."

The concierge bowed. "Mr. Aspen is expecting you. Right this way, sir."

Basil waved for Ginger to step in front of him, letting the rest of his group follow behind. Soon they were introduced to a private dining room decorated with wood, mirrors, white walls, and chandeliers, and brightened with large green potted palms in the corners.

Three men and a lady stood about casually. The lady and two of the men held glasses of champagne, whilst the third man, who wore round spectacles with particularly thick lenses, sipped on coffee. The lady, with honey-blonde hair adorned with a glittering headband sprouting a feather, was a fresh face, but the men, though older now since his first case, Basil did recognise. The man of the hour, squinting through thick lenses, hurried over, his arm outstretched.

"Inspector Basil Reed!"

Basil chuckled as he accepted the handshake. "Aspen, so good to see you. And it's Chief Inspector now."

"Yes, I knew that," Aspen said genially. "Old habits die hard."

Aspen was heftier and stronger than Basil remembered, likely a result of the physical demands of adventure travel. His dirty-blond hair was thinner, his forehead looked taller, and his thick spectacles made his dark eyes bigger. Basil wondered if he would've passed the man on the street.

"Travel appears to have been good for you," he said.

"Indeed, when I was last in London, a strong wind could've knocked me over." Aspen pushed up on his spectacles, then settled his gaze on Ginger. "Don't tell me this is your lovely lady?"

"Allow me to introduce you," Basil said with a note of pride. "Ginger, this is Mr. Aspen. Aspen, my wife, Mrs. Reed."

"You're a lucky man, Chief Inspector," Aspen said as he took Ginger's hand.

Basil introduced the rest of his family, although strangely, Cornelius hadn't yet arrived in the room. Even though Basil had informed Aspen of their number, the man seemed to greet them with slight apprehension, soon overridden with a smile.

Aspen introduced his early guests: Miss Helen Burton, a pretty if unoriginal bright young thing, who clung possessively to Aspen's arm. A banker, Mr. Ernest Yardley, whose name befitted his earnest demeanour, and a Fleet Street reporter, Mr. Cecil Lawrence, a man of limited stature who looked up at all the women in the room. Basil's mind registered the last meeting he'd had with each man; however, neither made mention of an earlier acquaintance, and Basil saw no reason to dredge up the past.

"Mr. Aspen," Charles began, "Basil has told us that you are somewhat a man of adventure."

"Oh, I've had my fun, I suppose, my Lord," Aspen returned, adding, as if he were keen to change the subject, "Now, please, everyone, enjoy your champagne. Or if you'd rather something different," he raised his coffee cup, "just let the waiter know."

The time for mingling had passed before more than superficial conversation could transpire when the head waiter, Evans, informed Aspen that dinner was ready to be served.

Towards the back of the room was a long table set with a white linen tablecloth. It appeared that Evans had taken the time to create seating cards, which prevented any awkwardness when it came to claiming one's seat.

The lights flickered on and off, causing the ladies to twitter and prompting everyone to make haste. With the tradition of alternating men and women and separating married couples, the placing went as follows: Aspen at the head of the table with Felicia, the lady with the highest title, at his right, then Basil, Ambrosia, Yardley, and Sally, with Lawrence at the end, then

Louisa, Gastrell, Ginger, Charles, and finally Miss Burton at Aspen's left.

Two waiters attended, pouring glasses of wine, after which Aspen tapped his fork against a glass, indicating he'd like to make a speech. Basil leaned in, curious as to why his old acquaintance had gathered them there.

Aspen repeatedly cast glances at Gastrell, who seemed to lean back slightly as if he expected Ginger's slight frame to shield him.

"Have we met before?" Aspen asked.

Gastrell pushed his lips out as he shook his head. "I dunno. I've got a face that often reminds people of someone else."

Aspen pushed up his heavy spectacles, a look of dismay on his face. Basil could only assume the man's poor eyesight caused him plenty of aggravation. Perhaps that was why he'd returned to London. A blind man might find comfort in his childhood home rather than the uncertainty of jungles and new vistas.

"Ladies and gentlemen," Aspen began, "it does my heart good to see you all here tonight. Miss Burton and I are in town for a very short visit, and although it was a bit of a mad scramble to contact you all, I thank you all for making an effort.

"I'm especially delighted that Chief Inspector Reed was able to bring his family." He squinted in

Basil's direction. "I'd heard news that you were doing well, and now I'm here to witness it for myself." He took in the rest of the table. "I look forward to perhaps someday getting to know all of you better."

Basil lifted his glass. "Hear, hear."

"And I understand you must be keen to learn why I've returned to London and gathered you here. Though I'm pleased to see new friends, this meeting is intended for my old ones, so allow me to assuage your curiosity." He paused, pinching his eyes closed as the lights flickered on and off, then said, "I'm here because I need your help."

4

*B*asil Reed stood in front of the main entrance of the South Building, otherwise known as "Scotland House", across the road from the Victoria Embankment. The impressive-looking redbrick building, banded with smart-looking white Portland stone, filled him with a sense of pride. He thought certain kinds of pride were good as he took off his hat and rubbed a hand through his wavy brown hair. He put his hat under his arm and walked through the doors with "New Scotland Yard" on them, painted in gold.

A young constable dressed in a dark blue uniform greeted Basil in the entrance lobby. "Good morning, Inspector."

"Good morning, Constable," Basil said, a smile twitching. It seemed surreal that he was entering the headquarters of the Metropolitan Police as a fully fledged inspector

A dull but all-too-familiar pain in his left side throbbed as he walked, a reminder of why a quick climb in ranks had been possible. A German bullet to the spleen whilst fighting at Ypres had taken him out of the military for good. Those months lying on his back in a London Hospital had slowly brought a new revelation to him. If he couldn't be a fighting man in France, he would enter training for the rank of police inspector and do his utmost to become the best damn crime solver Scotland Yard had ever seen.

The shame that came with sitting out the war whilst most of his comrades were giving their all for king and country was alleviated somewhat by his return to the Met and this new, if rather lofty, determination. It was a way to do his "bit".

"A very good morning to you, Inspector," another constable said as he passed Basil in the stairwell on his way up to the second floor. The usual discomposure one felt at being the new man on the floor was quickly dispelled by the acceptance Basil felt from his fellow policemen in the building.

Then there was Chief Inspector Morris.

"Inspector Reed," came the familiar booming voice from the far end of the hallway. The overbearing figure of the chief inspector appeared in a doorway, his beefy hand waving a clipboard. "About time, man."

Basil's jaw clenched. A glance at his wristwatch confirmed that he had not only arrived on time but was early by a full fifteen minutes.

"Please drop whatever you had planned for this morning and come into my office," Morris said gruffly.

"Yes, sir," Basil said, making a show of looking at his watch again. "I'll just hang my overcoat up before my shift starts." Basil wanted to emphasise that he had arrived early for work, not late as Morris had loudly and publicly insinuated. He might have been Basil's superior, but that didn't mean Basil was about to let the rather ungracious man shove him about.

Morris grunted, then disappeared into his office.

Precisely twelve minutes later, Basil sat across from Morris sans overcoat. He crossed his legs, a hot cup of tea in hand.

Morris scowled as he tapped his pen on his desk. "Are you quite comfortable, Inspector?"

"Quite," Basil said simply.

"Is the lighting all right for you?" Morris added more sarcasm as he gestured to the window that overlooked the footbridge separating the South Building from the North. "I could pull back the curtains a little more."

"No need," Basil returned. "The lighting is sufficient."

"What a relief!" Morris offered a disingenuous smile. "Now then," he said with a sniff. He pulled out a large manila envelope from his desk drawer and slid it towards Basil. "The superintendent wants you to have this assignment. A test, if you will, to prove you have what it takes to be an inspector." The side of his mouth drew up. "You're to report to me directly instead of the super. He's busy on several other cases, and as you know, the war has left us somewhat short of personnel."

"Yes, sir," Basil said, suppressing the disdain he felt for Morris, a man who most in the force believed hadn't earned his position but had gained it through opportunistic relationships.

"I received this file from the Deputy Assistant Commissioner himself," Morris said. "We want you to snoop around a bit and find information on suspicious activities by a business called Jennings Textiles in the East End. We have reason to believe the company may have been set up to swindle goods from textile suppliers. In fact, it may be just another iteration of criminal enterprises set up for such purposes."

Basil flipped through the file. "This activity isn't recent?"

"No. This may have been going on for several years

under different company names. The Yard has received a series of complaints over the last three years that are suspiciously consistent. It could be that there is an individual or a group of individuals setting up these nefarious companies all over London for cheating suppliers out of goods."

"Long firms," Basil commented.

Morris jutted out his chin. "What's that?"

"Long firms, sir. It's a term used to describe fake companies set up for shorter periods, but sometimes up to a year."

Morris stared at Basil with a blank expression. "So?"

"They gain the trust of suppliers until they finally make a large purchase of goods on credit. Then they simply disappear with those goods and sell them quickly for very discounted prices. They pocket the money and dispense it without any notion of ever paying back the debt. Often, they'll garner the cooperation of a successful businessman in the area, either with large bribes or by the threat of violence. Sometimes both."

"Well, I don't know how you know all that . . ."

"There were several cases in Manchester and Liverpool a few years back."

"Be that as it may . . ." Morris pulled down on his waistcoat, which had crept up over a rounded stomach.

"Whatever the game is, you need to find out the person or persons responsible and gather evidence against them."

It was a daunting task, but Basil was up for it.

"Yes, sir. I'll start immediately."

5

*M*r. Aspen pushed on his spectacles, looking uneasy as he gazed at his guests. "It seems I have an enemy. I've come back to London because I'm in fear for my life." He cleared his throat. "Forgive me for sounding melodramatic, and perhaps I'm being overly cautious if not a little paranoid . . ."

Before Mr. Aspen could finish explaining his situation and what he'd hope to gain from the company he'd gathered, a strange look suddenly crossed his face.

Ginger guessed the distraction was a woman in her mid-thirties, with dark curls pinned back with sparkly hair pins, round gold-framed spectacles on a Roman nose, and an eye-catching beauty mark—a dark mole on her right cheek. She stood at the entryway, staring intently at Mr. Aspen, with a hand on the hip of a stunning low-waisted frock.

"Percy, love," she said sweetly. "Don't you recognise your Winifred?"

Mr. Aspen pushed on his spectacles as he stammered, "W . . . Winifred?"

One corner of the lady's mouth turned up into a coy smile. "Yes, it's me. A little bird told me you were in town."

Ginger had to admire the lady's nerve. She had not only arrived apparently uninvited, she strolled brazenly to Mr. Aspen, causing him to jump to his feet. The woman grabbed his cheeks with two gloved hands and, rather solidly, kissed him on his long forehead.

"It's been donkey's years!" the new arrival said. And, as if she had only just become aware of the spectacle she'd created, she addressed the room.

"You must forgive my exuberance. My name is Miss Winifred Chapman. Percy and I have known each other for a long time." She shot him a flirtatious wink that had the effect of buckling poor Mr. Aspen's knees.

The shock on Miss Burton's face flattened then folded into a scowl. Mr. Yardley's jaw dropped, snapped, closed, and opened again. "Aspen?"

Ginger felt sympathy for their host. What was he to do? Presumed propriety on his part required that he offer an invitation, something Miss Chapman was no doubt counting on. He removed his spectacles, used his handkerchief to give the lenses a quick swipe, then put them on again. "Forgive me, Winifred; I'm just astounded to see you again."

Miss Chapman's eyebrow arched slightly as she carefully removed her white gloves, peeling them off inside out, and dropped them into her handbag. "I'm certain you are."

The table had been set for twelve, and on seeing Miss Chapman hovering, a waiter breezed in. "Shall I set another place?"

Cornelius guffawed loudly. "In Alabama, a pretty lady like Miss Chapman wouldn't be kept waiting." He rose, motioning to his chair.

"Don't be silly, Cornie," Louisa said, looking rather protective of her man. "She can sit beside me." On her feet now, Louisa waited as the waiter shifted her chair closer to Cornelius' and then provided another chair. Miss Chapman wasted no time in accepting it.

"Thank you," she said.

Mr. Aspen finally found his footing and made a quick round of introductions. "Miss Chapman and I are old friends."

"And yet you forgot to send me an invitation!" Miss Chapman's tone was light, but her eyes were sharp. "Perhaps it was lost in the post." She leaned in, capturing everyone's attention. "Once upon a time, we had an *understanding*. But then, poof. Percy disappeared."

Ginger stilled along with the rest of the group, who seemed frozen with disapproval and embarrassment.

"Winifred!" Mr. Aspen said.

Miss Chapman laughed. "It's quite all right. Water under the bridge and all that." She smiled coolly. "I came so we could be friends again, that's all. But, oh dear." Miss Chapman made a show of counting the guests. "I've made the number thirteen." She pouted. "So unlucky."

"Oh no," Miss Burton burst out. "You're right. We must get the cat!" She flapped her fingers at the waiter who lingered in the corner. "The cat, the cat!"

"Good golly," Sally scoffed. "Don't tell me Miss Burton is superstitious?"

"A lot of people are, Mother," Louisa said. "You won't find me walking under a ladder."

The waiter had jumped to attention, first bringing an extra chair and placing it opposite Miss Chapman.

"What's happening?" Ambrosia asked.

"It's for Kaspar the cat," Ginger started. "Number fourteen."

A waiter scurried over with a life-size statue of a black cat sitting on its back legs, its pointy feline nose tilted down and a long tail curling up.

"He's a handsome fellow," Miss Chapman said, "isn't he?"

A place setting had been provided for both Miss Chapman and Kaspar the cat. Then drinks were topped off all around.

Sally took a long sip of her wine then said, "Someone has to tell us the story behind this."

"Before the turn of the century," Ginger began, "a prominent businessman by the name of Woolf Joel frequented the Savoy. On one occasion, when his party was made up of fourteen guests, one of them cancelled at the last minute, leaving them with thirteen. Before the meal was over, Mr. Woolf rose to leave the table but was admonished that the first guest to leave a table of thirteen would be the first to die."

"Don't tell me," Cornelius said with a look of scorn. "He left, and he died."

"He did leave," Ginger said, holding her gaze with the rude man. "And later became a murder victim. After that, diners were fearful of making large reservations at the Savoy, so not long ago, an artist was employed to solve the problem by creating Kaspar. Now, if ever a party finds themselves at thirteen, Kaspar makes up the fourteenth place."

"No one here has left the table, have they?" Miss Burton said, her voice sounding a little too hopeful. "Before the cat was presented?"

Before anyone could reassure Mr. Aspen's lady friend, the lights flickered again, but instead of gradually brightening, they went out completely, drowning the room in blackness. Soft expressions of disapproval were emitted before one blood-curdling scream.

Cornelius' low-toned voice blurted out, "What the blazes?"

The lights flickered on again, and Ginger braced herself for the worst, twisting her torso, searching for Miss Chapman three chairs to her left. She was still very much alive, her eyes blinking with the rest of them as they adjusted from darkness to light.

Miss Burton exhaled harshly, her hands at her throat. "I'm sorry I screamed. I thought I felt something run across my foot and grab my neck."

"I may have accidentally kicked you," Charles said. "My apologies."

"And it was my arm searching for you, love," Mr. Aspen said.

"Much ado about nothing," Ambrosia muttered. "Once again."

Mr. Aspen had ordered a roast goose for dinner beforehand, and Ginger was grateful when the waiters brought the food to the table. After a starter of split-pea soup, the goose, carved with piles of white and dark meat separated onto two platters, was offered, along with fragrant sautéed wild mushrooms, roast potatoes and carrots, and creamy-brown gravy. Everyone was dished out an equal portion, including Kaspar the Cat. Ginger wondered who would benefit from a free meal afterwards. Hopefully, it wasn't to be wasted and tossed into the rubbish bin.

"Now that dinner has arrived," Mr. Aspen said, "I'll continue with my tale once we've finished eating."

Ginger's curiosity was definitely piqued, and she felt like she did when finishing a book that ended in suspense—frustrated and impatient. Conversation settled into a well-mannered, civilised affair, even between Basil and Cornelius, who insisted on making across-the-pond comparisons.

Then Miss Burton screamed again. "Percy! Percy? What's wrong?"

Percy Aspen, his face red and cheeks bulging, grabbed at his throat, knocking his spectacles off.

"Aspen!" Basil shouted and jumped to the man's aid, but in the short time it took to reach him, he'd slumped off his chair and onto the floor.

Oh mercy.

6

Ginger didn't have official medical training, but her time in France and Belgium during the war had made her a quick study on many things, and one thing was how to determine if a fallen soldier was alive or dead. Only she and Charles had rushed to join Basil.

Miss Burton seemed frozen to the spot, her red lips open in a silent scream.

Looking embarrassed for his friend, Mr. Yardley said, "Aspen, old chap! Do right yourself."

"Is he choking?" Mr. Lawrence offered, his eyes glimmering with interest, as another man's calamity could be a paying story for him.

To Basil, Ginger said, "Prop up his head."

Basil cupped the man's forehead and back of the head, lifting it, giving Ginger access to the loosening skin of his pale neck. The cacophony of voices continued as she pressed two fingers to Mr. Aspen's jugular vein.

"Gol dang it," Cornelius bellowed. "Can't you see the man's choking?"

"Mr. Aspen wouldn't immediately pass out from choking," Charles replied.

Louisa, gripping the long rope of pearls around her neck, offered, "Heart attack, then?"

"Oh, for heaven's sake," Sally blustered. "Stop guessing. You know nothing about medicine."

Basil gave Ginger a questioning look. She shook her head. "No pulse."

Putting his arms under Mr. Aspen's Basil lifted him onto the floor. "We must try to revive him."

"Pump his chest," Ginger said. She'd read up on the recent advancement of pulmonary resuscitation. "It'll keep the blood flowing to his brain."

Basil ripped off his jacket, leaned over the man, and began the rhythmic pumping with one hand clamped over the other.

Cornelius shouted, "What in Hades is he doing?"

Miss Burton found her voice, shrill with hysteria. "Is he dead?"

Miss Chapman was on her feet. "He has an allergy to seafood. Don't tell me he ate some shellfish!"

"We all ate the same thing," Mr. Lawrence returned.

Mr. Yardley's skin had turned a pumice-green. "Perhaps we should summon a doctor?"

Charles was halfway across the room. "I'm doing that now."

Ambrosia's hand went to her throat, the gems on her gnarly fingers catching the candlelight.

Felicia reached over Basil's empty seat to take her hand. "Are you all right, Grandmama?"

"It's not the first time I've dealt with death." Ambrosia looked more put out than traumatised. "I had a feeling I should've stayed in tonight."

Mr. Aspen, his pallor a ghostly white and his lips blue, wasn't responding to Basil's tireless effort. Ginger put a hand on her husband's shoulder. "Love, he's gone. I'm sorry."

Remaining on his haunches, Basil rubbed his eyes. "It's just so strange that he should die suddenly on the night of reunions." His gaze moved to the people at the table, and Ginger's eyes followed his. Besides Mr. Apsen's companion Miss Burton, Basil had been specially invited along with Mr. Lawrence and Mr. Yardley, the former busy scribbling in a notebook and the latter staring hard at the cloth napkin he twisted tightly in his hands.

Then there was the surprise attendee, Miss Chapman, whose face was a mask of non-expression, a startling contrast to her previous vivacious performance.

Charles returned with the announcement that an ambulance was on its way. Ginger approached him and Felicia. "Would you mind taking Ambrosia and our guests back to Hartigan House?"

"That would be appreciated," Ambrosia said.

Seemingly ready to leave the macabre affair, Sally and Louisa gathered their handbags.

"Leave now?" Cornelius protested. "This is the most interesting event since I got to this suffocating island."

"Cornie!" Louisa said. "A man has died."

"That's exactly what I mean."

Charles stepped over to Cornelius' side. "I implore you to leave without making a scene." With his determined gaze and the firm set of his jaw, Charles had an authoritative presence that even the stubborn and belligerent Cornelius Gastrell couldn't resist.

Mr. Yardley pushed away from the table. "Perhaps it's best if we all leave."

Basil, on his feet now, shook his head. "I'd rather you didn't, Mr. Yardley. I'd like to speak to each of you before you leave."

Mr. Lawrence blew through his lips. "*What*? You can't think any one of us has something to do with this? The poor bloke had a stroke."

"All the same," Basil said. "I'd like to wait for the doctor to arrive if you don't mind."

Both Mr. Lawrence and Mr. Yardley looked like they minded. Poor Miss Burton sniffed into a handkerchief as she stared blankly at the ceiling, her grief appearing to be more for herself and her change of circumstance than for the gentleman lying dead on the floor. Whimpering, she said, "But the cat was with us. How could this have happened?"

Commotion filled the room as Charles directed Ambrosia, Felicia, Sally, Louisa, and the reluctant Cornelius out the door, just as the attending doctor arrived.

"Dr. Kirk," he said as an introduction.

"I'm Chief Inspector Reed," Basil said, "here as a guest of the deceased and not in an official capacity. This is my wife, Mrs. Reed."

The doctor was already on his knees, his black bag on the floor and opened. "What happened?"

"As the lights have been flickering on and off most of the night, we hardly saw what happened until it was too late," Basil explained.

"He slumped over to the side," Ginger added, "his face barely missing his dinner plate."

"Did he show any signs of distress beforehand?" the doctor asked.

Miss Burton answered weakly. "He stiffened and gasped."

"Indeed," Mr. Yardley started. "His hand went to his throat."

"Mr. Lawrence?" Basil prompted. "Did you witness anything?"

After a shrug, the newspaperman said, "I was busy enjoying the roast."

The doctor ran through a preliminary examination of the body. "No apparent physical contusions."

"Naturally," Mr. Lawrence said with a scoff. "It's not like one of us hit him on the head during a short and unscheduled blackout."

"No one is suggesting foul play," Ginger said calmly. She took in the long, mostly empty table. It was only then that she realised that Miss Chapman was missing. She must've shuffled out with the rest when Ginger's back had been turned.

7

*B*aby Rosa was a good sleeper, but Ginger still wanted to be alerted if she awoke and couldn't quickly be pacified, which was why a tapping on her bedroom door awakened her just before dawn.

Ginger attributed it to natural maternal instincts that she could sleep soundly through a storm or Basil's snoring but woke immediately to Nanny's soft knock. Slipping out of bed, Ginger felt eager to hold her baby and surprised the nanny by opening the door with enthusiasm.

"She's awake, madam, and not ready to go back to sleep."

"That's all right, Nanny. I'm happy to take her. You can go back to sleep."

"Thank you, madam." The nanny, dressed in a long nightdress, dressing gown, and nightcap, handed

Rosa over, bowed slightly, and headed back across the corridor to the nursery.

Rosa whimpered, and Ginger whispered, "Shhh," as she found her rocking chair. Her eyes were now used to the new dawn light. Soon Rosa was happily nursing at her breast. Ginger was pleased that her little daughter had taken to the bottle as well, which made leaving her a little easier.

Basil shifted to his side, the early morning light streaming from the window and highlighting his face. He was getting older, as they all were, but Ginger found her heart warmed towards him with the same intensity it had when she'd first realised she'd fallen in love.

Never in her wildest dreams had she imagined, especially on the voyage from Boston in the summer of '23, that she'd remain mistress of Hartigan House, marry a good and handsome man, and be the mother of two wonderful children.

Her mind immediately went to Scout. He didn't seem to be adjusting well to boarding school, and Ginger was torn between bringing him home—she so missed the energy he brought to the house—and giving him a good and proper education.

Rosa gurgled, and Ginger propped her over her shoulder to rub her back.

"You're so very beautiful," Basil's voice came. "Like the Madonna."

"I didn't mean to wake you, love," Ginger said.

Basil sat upright. "It's a privilege to wake to such a sight. Besides, I'm needed at the Yard."

"Percy?" Ginger asked, knowing that Basil felt uneasy about the previous night's events. Something didn't sit right with her, and she'd suggested they get an official cause of death. Basil had agreed. "When is the autopsy being performed?"

"Hopefully this afternoon." Ginger watched as her husband crawled out of bed, stretched in his wrinkled pyjamas, then left the room for the bathroom. She continued nursing, pondering the events from the night before.

Ginger realised she knew little about her husband's life as a young police officer, a vocation his parents had never supported as they felt police work fell beneath his station in life.

When Basil returned, face clean and shaved, he reached out his arms for Rosa.

As Ginger handed the baby over, she said, "Tell me about the case?"

Basil gently rocked Rosa in his arms, staring at their daughter's big round eyes. He interrupted his cooing noises to say, "The case?"

"The one that drove Percy Aspen to abandon his

lady friend, Miss Chapman, and catch the first ship abroad?"

Basil's gaze darted from Rosa to Ginger, his brows raised. "That was a long time ago."

"I know," Ginger returned, "but I'd love to hear about it."

8

*B*asil spent most of the day at his desk, going through the files Morris had given him. There were several complaints going back to 1913 from materials' suppliers of all sorts. Setting up interviews with complainants would take effort. Basil hadn't any real experience in business, having never really run one.

When Basil had announced he was joining the police force, much to his father's dismay, the Honourable Henry Reed had turned an unhealthy crimson. The work was unfit for members of the peerage or their children. Chasing criminals was the job of commoners, a word his father used with the same tone he'd used when referring to goats.

If Basil wanted to enter the workforce, he should aspire to business. His father's estate managed several businesses, and Basil could have his pick. But Basil could be as stubborn as his father and put his heels in, and had entered police training two years earlier at the age of thirty-one after being invalided out of the war. Coming from a monied background meant that Basil would never have to worry about low police wages. Basil refused to show an interest in his father's businesses and therefore the whole concept was a bit of a mystery him.

And now, here he was, officially tasked with solving a business crime. Wouldn't good old dad laugh at that?

The London Library was a short bus ride away, and Basil thought he'd benefit by studying up on business basics. The chief librarian directed him to the reference books on subjects like supply chains, business law, and basic accounting.

Before the library closed, Basil signed out two volumes of recently written material about business strategies of successful London businesses. Racing to catch the next motorbus, he dodged a horse-drawn cart and distracted pedestrians crossing the roads hither and thither, hopping aboard the double-decker just in time.

Basil had the privilege of living on the edge of the well-to-do Mayfair district with his wife of four years, Emelia. He wished he could say they were happily married, but that would be a bold-faced lie. Emelia was the restless sort with a wandering heart and had broken his by having an affair with a veterinarian whilst Basil was on the continent fighting for his life.

With tears and desperate pleas, she had offered her apologies, and Basil had extended his forgiveness. But the doubts regarding her faithfulness remained. Perhaps, over time, their love would conquer all, and the betrayal would be forgotten.

Reaching his townhouse, Basil stepped in ie. "Darling, I'm home."

"In the sitting room, Basil."

The sitting room was a comforting mix of wood and light. A stone fireplace along one wall had warm coals, a remnant of a recent fire. On the wall hung a Waterhouse called Destiny. Basil had purchased the painting because the dark-haired beauty wearing a vivid red dress reminded him of Emelia. His wife hadn't shared his enthusiasm over the artwork, but put up little resistance when he hung it where it was often seen.

"How was your first day as inspector?" she asked.

"I've already been assigned an important investigation."

"Umm," she said, her focus back on the post.

"How was your day?" Basil asked in return. He placed his library books on the low table in front of the sofa.

"Oh, you know," she said as she took another letter

and opened it with the ivory-handled letter opener. "The usual."

"Oh, come now," Basil said. "Every day can't be exactly the same."

She shot him a look. "The weather is dreadful, with more rain in the forecast, and the war is still grinding on. Our prime minister seems intent on sending most of our male population to die in some godforsaken field of mud. I swear, one day, we shall be bereft of anybody except those men less than able-bodied."

The remark was like a cold stab.

"Oh, I'm sorry, Basil," she said without looking at him. "You know I don't mean you. You understand my point."

Basil swallowed the anger he felt rising and changed the subject, something he found himself doing more often these days.

"Did you get out at all today?" He removed his suit jacket, turning when he didn't get a response. "Emelia?"

His wife's face had suddenly turned pale. "On no," she said weakly.

"What is it?"

"This is from Elsa Wright."

Basil's heart skipped a beat. Elsa was the wife of his good friend Clive. "Is Clive all right?"

Emelia dropped the letter and stared.

"Has Clive been wounded?" Basil's voice choked.

He and Clive had been school chums, volunteering to join the forces on the same day. Basil had come home, leaving Clive to fight on. "Emelia?"

She just shook her head.

The truth hit hard. Clive had been lost.

An hour later, Basil sat in his study, a glass of whisky in hand.

Blast it. This deuced war and all the innocents it was claiming! What could he do? Drowning in drink wouldn't help Clive or any of those poor sods living in misery in the trenches. Be a bloody good copper, that was all he could do.

Basil took another long drink, his eyes focused on the first page of one of the library books, which Emelia had fastidiously relocated to his desk. With the back of his hand, he wiped his eyes, now blearing from tears and alcohol. One of the contributors to the book was a name that stirred his memory, Roland Wilcox.

Where had he seen that name?

Then, like a cloud slowly moving to reveal the sun, he remembered. Mr. Wilcox was listed as one of the complainants of the suspected long firm fraud, one of the more recent complainants.

"September 1915," Basil muttered aloud.

In the morning, he would track down this Mr. Wilcox. He was as good a place to start as any.

9

*E*nthralled by Basil's story as a new inspector, Ginger was disappointed that he had to leave without finishing. And what, if anything, did that old case have to do with what happened the evening before to poor Mr. Aspen?

Ginger was in her study, sitting at her desk under the pretext of having work to do. Sally, Louisa, and Cornelius were sightseeing again. Ginger had politely declined an invitation to join them, having had her fill of Cornelius through a shared breakfast. And with Basil at the Yard, Rosa having her morning nap, Scout away at boarding school, and Felicia married and busy with her new husband, Ginger felt restless. At least Boss remained, curled up in his bed by the fireplace.

Her work came in owning and running a thriving Regent Street dress shop called Feathers & Flair, and around the corner from that, the office of Lady Gold Investigations. When Rosa was born, Ginger had officially put her investigative business on indefinite hold. Now, having decided on the spring fashion line with her resident designer, Emma, Ginger had only a few letters to write and telephone calls to make. Her staff at the shop were so efficient, particularly her manager, Madame Roux, that it practically ran itself.

Ginger pushed away from her desk. "Bossy, would you like to go for a motorcar ride?"

In an instant, her Boston terrier was fully awake and standing, his little stubby tail wagging. "I've been thinking of my old friend Dr. Gupta. Shall we go and see what he's been up to lately?"

After letting Nanny know she was stepping out, Ginger put on a long plaid jacket with low front pockets, and a matching hat, along with her gloves, and then picked up a black-leather handbag. She reviewed her appearance in the entrance mirror and made a minor adjustment to her hat. One never knew who one would run into, and it didn't hurt to look one's best.

With Boss on her heels, she used the back garden exit and took the short, cobbled path to the garage that housed her pearly-white 1924 Crossley. She waved at her sturdy gardener. "Good morning, Clement!"

"Good afternoon, madam."

Clement opened the garage door for Ginger and

waited for her to start the engine and back out. With Boss happily in the passenger seat, a rich cherry-red leather, Ginger succeeded at her task with only one loud grinding of the gears and a few jerks as she misread the clutch. Once on the road, she fared much better, having grown accustomed to the frequent honking that followed her along the streets of London. Londoners weren't known for their patience and, with the advent of the motor car, had become increasingly irritated. At least Ginger thought so.

Travelling by way of Marylebone Road, Ginger cut through Park Square. By the time she'd arrived at the University College Hospital, she was astounded that her white spoked tyres remained intact. Negotiating the plethora of potholes found in London's narrow and meandering streets was no small feat.

Regardless, Boss enjoyed himself and happily waited for Ginger to secure a leash to his collar. She'd learned to take the back entrance to the basement level of the mortuary when she had Boss with her. The caretaker never minded her pet, and as for the others, her oversized coat gave her the means to conceal him.

Ginger knocked on the mortuary door before entering, and on hearing Dr. Gupta call for her to enter, did so. The mortuary in the hospital's basement was painted white to make the most of the new electric lighting, with tile floors, shelves, and cabinets containing every apparatus and chemical that excited scientists. A ceramic surgical table sat in the middle of the room; large round lamps hung from the ceiling above it. On the back wall, a row of relatively new refrigerated cabinets held the deceased until they were transported to the undertakers.

Dr. Gupta, a handsome Indian man, smiled at her. "Mrs. Reed. I suppose I shouldn't be surprised."

"Why do you say that?" Ginger said. "You've been on my mind, and since I'm often in the area, I thought I should drop in and see how my old friend is doing."

"Of course," Dr. Gupta said graciously. "Do forgive me. My wife and son are terrific, and work is going well. How are you?"

"Very well, thank you." Ginger helped herself to an empty chair and plucked off her gloves, one finger at a time. "Little Rosa is growing so fast; she'll be sitting soon. And Scout is thirteen! At boarding school, like a lot of other lads his age. Poor thing's not adjusting well, but Basil says to give him time."

"And Mr. Reed?" Dr. Gupta asked with a glint in his eye.

"Oh, he's practically running the Yard. I've no doubt that he'll be superintendent one day."

"You have a lot of faith in me, love."

Ginger turned to the sound of her husband's voice. "Oh, hello, Basil. Fancy meeting you here."

Basil grinned. "Yes, fancy that."

Dr. Gupta laughed. "You two were really made for each other."

Ginger couldn't have agreed more. "Absolutely."

"It's a pleasure to see you again, Doctor," Basil said, "but as you know, this isn't a social call. I received word that you had a report for Percy Aspen."

"I do indeed." Dr. Gupta referred to a clipboard he picked up from a desk. "Mr. Percy Aspen died from a lethal dose of Lucineride."

"He was murdered?" Basil said.

Dr. Gupta nodded. "He was murdered."

Ginger stared at her husband. "Lucineride? It's been a while since I've heard that particular poison bandied about."

"I don't think I've ever heard of it," Basil said. "Is it rare?"

Dr. Gupta stroked his smoothly shaved chin. "Rather, but obtainable illicitly, if one has the right connections. It's unique in that it can be absorbed into the skin producing a lethal reaction. Most poisons are ingested or inhaled."

"You're saying a person need only have rubbed it into Percy's skin?" Basil asked with a note of disbelief.

"Theoretically," Dr. Gupta said. "Though it can be administered through the skin, it can also be ingested, with just a small amount put in one's food or drink, particularly a warm beverage like tea or coffee or mixed into a soup or gravy."

"We all had the same meal," Ginger said, "which included soup at the start and gravy later with the main course. If it was administered that way, it had to be by someone within an arm's reach."

"The lights were flickering regularly," Basil said. "An electrical issue the management confirmed had been a problem."

"The situation had been reported in the papers," Ginger added. "The perpetrator could've known this and come prepared."

"A well-thought-out murder," Basil agreed. "But by whom?"

"The most likely would be Helen Burton, Cecil Lawrence, or Ernest Yardley," Ginger said, "as they were present before the rest of us and had access to his drink."

"Indeed," Basil returned, then to Dr. Gupta asked, "Is there anything else you can tell us about Lucineride?"

"Only that, when cooled, it creates a colourless, slightly moist waxy substance. If it is applied externally, it dries very quickly once it is absorbed by the skin. The deadly symptoms disrupt the parasympathetic nervous system—involuntary activities such as sweating, heart rate, and breathing. This leads to a quick death if not treated."

"Do the effects begin immediately?" Ginger asked.

Dr. Gupta shrugged. "Not in most cases. It takes twenty to thirty minutes for the body to absorb it fully, but then, it works quickly."

"Is there an antidote?" Ginger asked.

"Yes," Dr. Gupta said with a quick nod. "However, it would need to be applied within minutes to be effective." At Ginger's look, he added, "I'll have the laboratory concoct a few doses as a precautionary measure."

Satisfied, Ginger turned to Basil. "Shall we begin with his close lady friend? She probably knew him better than the gentlemen at the dinner party."

"My thoughts precisely," Basil said as he slipped a hand into his coat pocket, removing a notebook. "I have an address for Miss Burton."

10

*G*inger drove with Basil in his forest-green 1922 Austin 7. Early in their relationship, Basil had gently hinted that he didn't care for Ginger's driving, but Ginger thought it had more to do with common masculine ego than her driving skills.

In cases like this, she didn't mind as it gave her licence to let her mind freely wander and, in particular, recall her impressions of Miss Burton and how she gazed at Percy Aspen with unabashed adoration. That he seemed to respond in kind made it clear to Ginger that the two had been in a sincere, romantic relationship. That, or one of them was a skilled performer.

Miss Burton was much younger; though Ginger could hardly judge her for that; there were ten years between herself and Basil. Ginger would guess there were twice as many years bridging Miss Burton and Mr. Aspen.

Basil pulled to the kerb in front of the building where Miss Burton lived and cut the engine of his Austin. "I do hope she's in."

Ginger hoped so too. Part of what made an exciting investigation a dreary experience was running into walls, especially missing persons of interest. However, they were satisfied as Miss Burton answered the door herself.

Compared with her presentation during the evening at the Savoy, Helen Burton's appearance was subdued: her face looked much younger without make-up, and she wore a simple day frock.

"Hello," she said weakly. "I wondered when someone from the police would call."

Basil removed his hat. "Might we come in?"

"Certainly." Miss Burton led them to the humbly furnished sitting room. Ginger had expected more from a lady friend of Percy Aspen, who was known to have money and thus, it could be presumed that most of his friends would be moneyed also. And if not friends, at least girlfriends, so one could be reassured that the romantic interest was genuine and that the lady wasn't simply after one's fortune.

This wasn't always the case.

Miss Burton disappeared momentarily, then returned. "Mother's preparing tea."

"Tea would be delightful," Ginger said, taking a seat. "We're very sorry to intrude on what must be a difficult day."

Sitting in a matching chair, Miss Burton produced a handkerchief from her dress pocket and sniffed. "I've wept out all my tears for the time being. I just can't believe this has happened. I can't believe Percy is gone! I'm just so unlucky!" A blank stare followed her grief. "Do you know what caused his death? Was it a heart attack?"

Basil shot Ginger a quick look before answering. "I'm afraid we're still waiting on answers from the pathologist, but we have reason to believe it may not be something as simple as that."

Miss Burton's forehead buckled. "I don't understand."

Without explaining, Ginger jumped in with the next question. "How long had you and Mr. Aspen been acquainted?"

"For a few months now. Since last autumn. We met on a ship and had been in a relationship since."

"As did we," Ginger said. "Mr. Reed and I met on a steamship travelling from Boston to Liverpool. What was your vessel's itinerary?"

"Rio de Janeiro to Lisbon, and then Southhampton."

"Miss Burton, do forgive my asking, but how did the two of you meet? It's my understanding that Mr. Aspen, since making his fortune, only travelled first class?"

Miss Burton bristled at the implication, her cheeks brightening. "I also travelled first class, a gift from my uncle. But to answer your question, we met through a mutual friend."

Basil leaned in with interest. "Who was this mutual friend?"

"Well . . ." Miss Burton became fascinated with her handkerchief and twisted it as if her life depended on the knot. "We weren't fast friends. I only met her on deck—a Miss Mary Jones. Look, as you can see, I'm not a woman with wealth of my own. I'm not academic, and I don't possess many skills. I don't have a lot to recommend me, and when Mother dies—"

Mrs. Burton entered the room at that moment. "I'm not going anywhere yet," she said stiffly. Leaving the tea for Miss Burton to pour, the older Burton lady left the room, her nose in the air.

Miss Burton sighed. "Please forgive her. She's just upset at Mr. Aspen's passing away."

Ginger began to understand. Percy was the golden ticket to raise these women out of a potential financially dire situation. Miss Burton's eyes failed to show sympathy as they followed her mother's retreat out of the room. Had she killed Percy out of a twisted sense of getting back at her mother for some imagined grievance? Perhaps she hadn't meant for the man to die.

Miss Burton poured tea for everyone. After the first sip, Basil lifted his chin. "Please continue with your story, Miss Burton. You were telling us about Miss Jones."

"Yes, she informed me that there was an eligible bachelor on board and that she could arrange for me to meet him. She even lent me a proper frock, the highest fashion, to increase my chances of catching his eye."

Ginger set her teacup on its matching saucer with a soft clink. "It appeared to have worked."

Miss Burton smiled, her eyes glinting with the look of the victorious. "Oh yes. By the time we reached Lisbon, I had him wrapped around my little finger."

"That hardly seems the stuff of true love," Basil said stiffly.

Miss Burton reverted to her role of grieving girlfriend. "Love can look different for different folks, Chief Inspector. We loved each other in our own ways. He could give me what I want, and I could give him," she winked at Basil, "what he wanted."

Ginger pushed back the alarm at Miss Burton's blatant flirtatiousness with Basil. She cleared her throat and said, "Why didn't Miss Jones pursue Mr. Aspen herself?"

Miss Burton's expression crumpled in confusion. "I can't say. She was a lovely lady if a bit plain. Percy may have been too old for her. And one did have to overlook his thick spectacles." She took a sip of tea before setting her cup and saucer on the table. "Now, if you don't mind, I'm feeling rather tired, and I have Mother to tend to."

"Thank you for your time, Miss Burton."

A sly smile preceded her coy response. "Any time, Chief Inspector."

Had Ginger been the jealous kind, she would've been livid. Instead, she laughed as they stepped outside.

Basil linked his arm in hers. "You could at least pretend to be affronted."

"That road goes both ways," Ginger said with a grin, just as a young man, a passenger in a sporty Mercedes-Benz, looked at her and tipped his hat.

11

*B*asil found Roland Wilcox in his office, nicely furnished for being in such an industrial building, on the top floor of the building housing a large manufacturing company in Dagenham. Wilcox, a gruff-looking company owner, stared through a large window to the floor below, where dozens of machines, the purpose of which Basil could only guess at, filled the huge room. A network of gears and pulleys was built into the high ceiling, and wide belts of canvas material led from there to more wheels and pulleys on machines bolted to the wooden floor. At least one employee manned each machine. Basil sniffed the air, which smelled of oil and dust.

In his early forties and a good three inches taller than Basil, Roland Wilcox was completely bald on top, with a crown of white hair from temple to temple, which tapered into large whiskers that extended down to his jowls.

"I inherited this business from me father," Wilcox explained. "Most of the time, there are two dozen men, including four apprentices, and six women workin' 'ere. And two other factories in London," he added with a note of pride. "Both in the East End and about the same size as this one."

"Impressive," Basil said with sincerity.

Wilcox hooked his thumbs on the braces that held up his trousers. "We supply parts for everythin' from the shipyards to motorcar manufacturin' to plumbin' fixtures. I don't have formal trainin' in engineerin', but I can design and make you almost anythin' out of iron, copper, or steel."

"I visited the library to familiarise myself more with your type of business," Basil said, "and I noticed that you're listed as one of the contributors to one of the more recent books entitled, 'Prominent Figures in London Manufacturing'."

"You did, eh?" Wilcox allowed a small smile to come to his lips. "Yeah, if my dear ol' dad knew I would be part of writin' a book about ownin' a factory, he would be buyin' a few rounds for his mates up in heaven, I'm sure. About five years ago, I was asked to contribute a few words before all this blasted fightin' in France." As if inspired by the concept of fighting, he made a show of opening his arms, rolling up his sleeves, and then crossing his arms again.

"The business wasn't farin' so well when dad handed it over to me. I built it up again through a mixture of luck and hard work. I suppose that's why them blokes at the publishin' house asked me to help out."

"Bravo," Basil said appreciatively, thankful for good editors. "Well done."

"I don't expect you came to talk about me accomplishments. What can I 'elp you with, Inspector?"

"According to police records, you were a complainant in a report on some bad goings on involving one of your former clients."

Wilcox scratched at one of his lamb-chop sideburns. "That was almost a year ago!"

"Yes, I know; however, I was just given the assignment yesterday. As you can imagine, this war has put a squeeze on the force."

"Yeah, like everythin' else. Don't get me wrong, Inspector. I would be the first to head to France and do me part for king and country, and so would any of me men here. But I'm thankful that the Military Service Act excludes those in our line of work. We'd be done if I had to send these men to war."

"Indeed."

"You seem like a fellow who's finally gonna get to

the bottom of it all." Wilcox held Basil's gaze. "You understand that this isn't somethin' that just happened to me."

"I do. There are several similar reports. Can you tell me what happened in your case?"

Wilcox fell into his desk chair with a plop, threaded his fingers, and settled them on a soft stomach. "Well, it's simple, Inspector. I was supplyin' parts to a respected distributor here in London."

Basil remembered the name from the police file—Douglas Industries.

"Yes, sir. Patrick Douglas distributed parts to ship-builders all around the coast. We sometimes use companies like that to get wider circulation for our products. It helps me stay focused on what I do best, which is designin' and buildin'." He let out a tired sigh. "Things were goin' well for about a year. Then, the company put a large order for engine parts, boiler parts, and gearin'—things of that nature. It was a huge order, but we were up to it. We worked day and night to meet the deadline, delivering all of it right on time. I didn't know that the owner of the company, Patrick Douglas, had quietly sold his company just after he put in the order. I thought I was dealin' with him the whole time, but it turned out I'd been dealin' with a group of thugs and charlatans who sold the parts at discounted prices in other cities."

"And then defaulted on payment," Basil said.

"Not only that, they disappeared! Two days after I delivered the whole lot. Unfortunately, I didn't find out about it until two months later. Finally, when I didn't get the payments as promised, I went to their office meself, only to find it no longer existed. Nearly did me in."

"Did you try to find Douglas?" Basil asked.

"Word on the street was that he'd moved to America. He and his wife, gone. No one knows where, and I don't 'ave the time to dig any further or money to chase him down."

Basil whistled. "Did you talk to Douglas's office-building owner here in London?"

Wilcox nodded deeply. "He told me a group of men had taken over the building lease."

"A group of men?"

"A group of scoundrels is what I say."

"Any idea who?"

"Like I said, Inspector, I don't have the time to be a detective. That's why I filed a complaint with Scotland Yard."

"I assume," Basil started, "that if this ever gets to court, you'd be willing to testify?"

"Ha! You can bet on that. And by the way, I do have one name."

Basil gave Wilcox his full attention, pen and notepad at the ready. "Yes?"

"Sharp. Mortimer Sharp. Word on the street is he's the mastermind behind this scheme."

"Hmm." Basil said, wondering how he could tap into the 'word on the street'. "I'm not familiar with that name."

"You can ask the other business owners who've been swindled. Mortimer Sharp is the name you'll be writin' down over and over again in that notepad of yours."

12

Ginger smoothed out her skirt as she settled into the passenger seat of Basil's Austin. Once Basil was seated beside her, she asked, "Who's next? Mr. Lawrence or Mr. Yardley?"

"Lawrence," Basil said as he started the engine. It turned over with a rumble, and he put it into gear as he craned his neck to ensure another motorcar, motorbus, horse and cart, or bicycle wasn't in his way. "Lawrence covered the story about the case Percy was involved with."

"Yes," Ginger said. "You never finished the story. What was the crime, exactly? Who was the perpetrator?"

"*Crimes,*" Basil emphasised. He turned the motorcar towards Fleet Street. "The man, a Mortimer Sharp, led a gangster ring before the war and was most definitely guilty of many crimes, from tax evasion to murder, though in the end, we got him on business fraud. He took a lot of innocent men to the cleaners."

"And how was Percy involved?"

"He was a new accountant at a firm used by several of Sharp's fake companies, the only one who refused to be bought out. He brought the falsified accounts to the police and remained under police protection until the trial. He had every reason to fear for his life, and I wasn't surprised when he left the country."

"Without Miss Chapman," Ginger added.

"Perhaps he feared for her life as well."

Ginger conceded it would be the noble thing to do, even if it were painful for the lady. "And the killer didn't want him to get that far." Ginger played with a lock of hair that stuck out from her hat. "What part did Mr. Lawrence play?"

Basil answered, "He covered the story, along with other reporters, but his pieces tended to water things down."

Ginger was aghast. "Favouring the gangsters?"

"Not blatantly. He had a way of reporting that suggested doubt, which worked for the defendants to create reasonable doubt. It worked most of the time."

"But not the last time," Ginger said. "Because of Percy."

"Exactly."

"So curious as to why Percy had invited Mr. Lawrence to the Savoy."

Basil pulled the Austin to a stop on Fleet Street in front of the London News Agency. "It's what I hope we'll find out by interviewing him."

The receptionist, a young woman who looked like she wasn't even twenty yet, said, "I'm sorry, but Mr. Lawrence isn't at his desk."

Ginger held in her disappointment as Basil asked, "When do you expect him to return?"

"I'm afraid he doesn't report to me." She rolled her eyes. "These journalists keep their own hours."

"We'll have to track Mr. Lawrence down later," Ginger said. "Mr. Yardley should be easier to track down."

The banker was indeed easier to find. He was seated behind his desk at Barclays, wearing a grey suit with a black tie. He smiled warmly until he recognised Ginger and Basil and realised they were not potential new customers approaching him.

"Chief Inspector Reed, Mrs. Reed. How may I be of service?" he added with a glimmer of hope in his voice. "Would you like to open an account?"

Basil motioned for Ginger to take one of the empty chairs, then took one for himself. "Not today, Mr. Yardley," Ginger said. "We're here with news of Mr. Aspen.

Since you were also his friend, we wanted to tell you in person."

Mr. Yardley tented his fingertips together. "Oh dear. This sounds serious."

"I'm afraid it's rather dire," Basil said. "You see, we've spoken to the pathologist this morning and were informed that Aspen had been poisoned."

After a hard swallow, Mr. Yardley gasped. "Poisoned? Are you sure?"

"Quite," Basil said. "As a result, I'm here on official police business. It's only coincidence that Mrs. Reed is with me."

Ginger played along. "I came to do some banking. My meeting up with my husband was pure serendipity. But now that I'm here, I would also like to know what you know about Percy Aspen." She cocked her head. "It might help me to console poor Miss Burton. She's very distressed, as you can imagine."

Mr. Yardley leaned back in his chair and crossed his arms, the folds of his suit jacket wrinkling at the elbows. "I can hardly imagine what you expect from me. I certainly didn't poison the man."

"Why were you invited?" Basil asked. "Had the two of you kept in contact whilst Mr. Aspen was travelling?"

"No, we hadn't corresponded at all," Mr. Yardley said, unfolding his arms. "And as to why I was invited to dinner, I have no idea. I simply accepted because I'd never dined at the Savoy before. You can believe I now wished I had declined."

Ginger was as puzzled as the banker seemed to be. "Are you familiar with the name Mortimer Sharp?"

Mr. Yardley exhaled slowly. "Mortimer Sharp? Oh yes, of course. The Sharp trial was in all the rags for weeks. But I never had any business with the man or his associates. Now, if you don't have any banking I can help you with, I'll ask that you leave." He pointed his chin to a couple seated nearby, waiting for him to become free.

Ginger and Basil rose.

"Thank you for your time, Mr. Yardley," Basil said.

"Not at all."

On the street, as they passed impatient pedestrians on the pavement, Ginger said, "I really wish Mr. Aspen had had time to explain what exactly he thought everyone could do to help him when he'd called you all together. It's still rather puzzling."

Basil opened the passenger door for Ginger. "You and me both, love. You and me both."

*a*fter Basil had dropped Ginger off at her Crossley, she decided on one last errand before heading back to Hartigan House: tracking down Miss Chapman.

Just as she was about to pull out onto the street, a black cat raced across, causing the motorcar coming from the opposite direction to slam on its brakes. The driver gave the rubber bulb of the horn three frustrated blasts.

As a Brit, Ginger saw the feline as a sign of good luck to come, but the American superstition about bad luck following when a black cat crossed one's path made her shiver involuntarily.

Ginger drove across the River Thames on the Albert Bridge, past Battersea Park, and soon approached a building comprising of flats in Clapham where many middle-class people lived. Normally, Ginger would've sent a messenger to announce her plans to visit, but since Miss Chapman wasn't a friend of hers, and since she'd found the element of surprise to work in her favour, Ginger knocked on the door and hoped for the best.

A female voice Ginger didn't recognise called from the other side of the door, "Who is it?"

"Mrs. Ginger Reed, looking for Miss Chapman."

"Oh." After a moment, the door opened, and a woman in her early twenties stood before Ginger. Her dull brown hair hung loose, framing a youthful face. Her short nose was quite noticeably sprinkled with freckles. "Aunt Winifred isn't feeling well," the young woman said. "Can I help you?"

"Miss Chapman is your aunt?" Ginger asked. "So, you must be?"

"Uh, Vera Chapman. I'm visiting."

"Your aunt and I met last night at the Savoy. I suppose she's mentioned the unfortunate circumstances?"

Vera nodded deeply. "Oh yes. A man *died*. How terrible!"

Ginger ducked her chin and lowered her voice conspiratorially. "I've learned something interesting that your aunt might be very interested in learning."

"Oh?" Miss Vera Chapman said. "What is it?"

"I'd rather speak to Miss Chapman about it," Ginger said. "It's rather delicate. Perhaps I'll come back later. Or she can ring me." Ginger dug through her handbag for a card.

"Let me see if my aunt is up to seeing you, Mrs. Reed," Miss Vera said, taking the bait Ginger had set out.

A person's curiosity is a strong motivator.

Miss Vera continued. "Please come in. Help yourself to a cup of tea. There's a pot in the kitchen. I've just made it. It may take Aunt Winifred a few minutes to revive."

Ginger poured her tea, added sugar, and sipped as she took in the place. Plainly outfitted, with a three-piece suite and matching cotton cushions, there was little to denote a personal touch—as if Miss Chapman had only just taken the flat already furnished.

Glancing at her wristwatch, a delicate Bulova made of etched white gold, Ginger noted that ten minutes had passed. The niece must be having a hard time rousing her aunt. Vera Chapman really wanted to know Ginger's news!

Finally, Winifred Chapman appeared and indeed looked under the weather.

"You must excuse my appearance, Mrs. Reed," she said with her characteristic low and raspy voice. "It must've been something I ate last night."

Ginger didn't bother pointing out that everyone was served the same meal at the Savoy as she watched Miss Chapman take her place at the table. There was a strong resemblance between niece and aunt, mostly in the eyes. The main differences were the nose and the hair and the distinctive mole belonging to the elder. Vera Chapman's nose was petite and had freckles, whereas Winifred's was more prominent. Winifred's skin was a shade darker and smoother.

"I'm sorry to drag you from your bed. I hope you don't mind me saying that you look rather under the weather."

"Not at all." Miss Winifred cupped her nose as if its bridge caused her nasal discomfort. "I'm curious as to how you found me?"

"You gave your address to the police."

"Ah, yes, I did." Miss Winifred's eyes flashed with disapproval. "It might surprise you by my performance last night, but I'm a rather private person. Unfortunately, I got into my cups early in the evening, and well, one never knows what one might do when one's mind isn't completely clear. Now, Vera says you have interesting news regarding Percy; God rest his soul."

"I do, and I know you and Mr. Aspen were once close, so I hope what I have to say isn't too distressing. Do you mind if I ask why you didn't go to South Africa with him?"

Miss Winifred let out a short breath. "If you must know, he didn't bother to ask me to join him. I would've said yes, but . . ." She waved a hand. "That's ancient history now. I've moved on."

Ginger wondered exactly how Miss Winifred had moved on. As far as Ginger knew, she'd never married, and therefore, never had children. "Do you have an occupation?" Ginger asked. "Women these days have more opportunities than our recent ancestors had. I run two businesses."

"Two! How enterprising. I'm not as ambitious as all that. I have my own income and divide my time between London and Bath, sometimes Edinburgh. Now, Mrs. Reed, please do release me from bitter suspense. What news do you bring?"

"I'm afraid it isn't good, Miss Chapman. My relationship with Scotland Yard and the hospital mortuary gives me access to some information before it's released to the public, so I must have your assurances that you'll not speak of what I'm about to tell you before the police do."

Miss Winifred mimicked locking her lips with an invisible key. "Do tell."

"Mr. Aspen was poisoned."

Miss Winifred lowered her teacup. "How shocking." Her hand reached for the collar of her blouse. "But how? Why?"

"These are questions for the police, I'm afraid," Ginger said. "Do you have any idea who might wish Mr. Aspen harm?"

"How should I know?" Miss Winifred twisted in her chair and crossed her legs. "I'd been out of touch with the man for ten years."

Ginger stated the obvious. "It's my understanding that you weren't invited. Why did you crash the dinner party?"

"You've seen what I'll do to assuage my curiosity, Mrs. Reed." Miss Winifred laughed hoarsely. "Rise from the dead, if need be. I simply needed to see him again. And yes, I felt a certain amount of satisfaction at shocking Percy like that. Compared with what he did to me, it was child's play."

"A bit of revenge," Ginger said.

"I suppose so."

"Perhaps you wanted to do more than just surprise Percy."

"You mean kill him?" Miss Winifred chortled. "And how did I manage to do that? You saw where I was seated. How would I have killed him?" She coughed into her fist, whether sincerely or for show, Ginger couldn't tell. "I'm no detective, but the person within arm's reach would be your best bet."

Ginger sipped the last of her tea. "I imagine you're

right about that, Miss Chapman. Anyone in particular?"

"You're asking me?"

"I'm curious who you think could do such a thing."

"Like a game, eh? All right, I'll play. Miss Burton, if she was growing weary of waiting for a wedding date. Believe me, she could have been waiting a long time." She snickered. "I guess she'll be waiting for the next fellow now."

"Not really a motive for murder, though, is it?" Ginger said. "If she wanted to hurry along the nuptials."

"Perhaps she didn't mean for him to die. Just to realise he didn't have all the time in the world."

"That's possible."

Miss Winifred pushed away from the table. "I appreciate you going out of your way to let me know, Mrs. Reed, but I really am feeling fatigued." She yawned for emphasis. "You don't mind seeing yourself out?"

"Not at all," Ginger said. "I hope you feel better soon."

14

*T*he offices of the London News Agency were on Fleet Street, and as Basil climbed the stairs to find the newsroom on the third floor, he pulled the name he had written on a piece of paper out of his breast pocket.

Upon enquiring at the reception counter, a pleasant clerk with the name of Jon Davids directed him to a desk on the far side of the busy room. Having encountered the newsman before as he had reported on previous cases Basil had worked on, Basil recognised the reporter at once. Cecil Lawrence was a diminutive man by anyone's standards. He was wearing a rumpled white shirt with an oversized black tie—at least it looked over-sized on him—and he couldn't have been more than seven and a half stone soaking wet. To compensate for his lack of stature, he wore a great, thick moustache, *waxed and twirled at the ends, so the ends poked out beyond the width of his face.*

He tapped away at a typewriter while carefully reading notes scrawled on a sheet of paper. Judging by how slowly he was typing, one index finger at a time, it would take him a while to transcribe the whole page.

When he noticed Basil, his thick eyebrows went up, and he stopped mid-stroke. He leaned back in his chair, invoking a loud creaking sound from it.

"Mr. Lawrence," Basil said as he came to stand in front of the cluttered desk.

"Sergeant Reed," Cecil Lawrence said as he drew himself up to his full height of five feet two inches and took Basil's offered hand.

"It's Inspector Reed now," Basil said.

"A promotion for you, eh? Jolly good. So, what can I do for you, Inspector?"

"I would appreciate a moment of your time if you can spare it."

"I can hardly say no to a Yardman." He gestured to an empty wooden chair. "Have a seat."

Basil took the proffered chair, saying nonchalantly, "Are you still enjoying London?"

"What do you mean? Oh, I see. You guessed I'm not from here." Lawrence stuck a hand-rolled cigarette between his lips and lit it. He motioned to Basil in a silent offer to join him.

Basil shook his head. "No, thank you."

"So, how'd you know?"

"Your Scouse accent slips through now and then and rather gives away that you're from Liverpool."

"Very good, Inspector. I moved here a few years ago when this position was offered to me."

Basil crossed his legs casually. "I read an article you wrote for the Liverpool Herald some time ago. You could call me a newspaper enthusiast. I have subscriptions to many. As a detective, it's good to be informed of cases in other cities. Sometimes patterns emerge that can be helpful in local crimes."

"I see." Mr. Lawrence blew smoke into the collective pool that gathered at the ceiling of the bullpen. "That's very interesting. But what does that have to do with me?"

"I'm working on a case that closely resembles a story you covered for The Herald."

Lawrence leaned in. "Oh? Which one is that then?"

"The business fraud. Long firm, they call it."

"Yeah," Lawrence said after a beat. "I remember it."

"The way it works, as I understand it," Basil continued, "is that an unscrupulous individual or a group of individuals buys out a business in midstream, so to speak. The transaction is achieved by using coercion or compensating the business owner handsomely for his part in it."

Lawrence placed his cigarette in an ashtray, creating a long piece of ash. "That's correct, Inspector. Sometimes the owner might end up doing time in prison, and the sum reflects that risk."

"And then, using the business's good reputation, they place a substantial order on credit, only they turn around and sell at discounted prices, and then disappear, leaving the manufacturer holding the cost for the goods."

"So, what can I help you with?" Lawrence said with a note of impatience. "You sound like you've got it all figured out."

"Have you ever come across the name Mortimer Sharp? Perhaps whilst covering a story in Liverpool?"

"Hmm. As I said, that was quite a while ago. No, that name's not ringing any bells." He folded his arms and leaned back.

Basil had been doing his job long enough to know when he'd caught a liar, and Lawrence was lying.

"Well, that's funny," Basil said, leaning in to close the gap Lawrence had created. "Because Mortimer Sharp is from Liverpool, and his name is associated with the business crimes you wrote about in Liverpool. It seems—"

"Well," the reporter lightly slapped his thigh, "I am not sure I recall any name like that."

Basil made a point of removing his notebook and

flipping pages. "Another newsman, an associate of yours, Mac Turnbull? Also covered the crimes."

"So? Anyway, he retired."

"Are you sure?"

Lawrence stared like a man who realised he'd just misstepped.

Basil continued, "You see, I rang the paper before coming here. Mac Turnbull does still work there but is on holiday right now. I'm told he's due back in a few days. Do you think he would remember the name of Mortimer Sharp?"

Lawrence's shoulders sagged as he exhaled slowly. "Look, Mortimer Sharp is a dangerous bloke. A mastermind, if you will. He's never been brought to trial, and with his pull, I doubt he ever will be. There's a trail of people afraid of their own shadow because of him, and I'm ashamed to say I am one of them. Off the record, I would never testify in court."

The reporter's honesty and his willingness to defy the law, to be found guilty of contempt and imprisoned, startled Basil. Just what kind of man was this Mortimer Sharp that he could inspire so much fear?

Basil let the silence grow and was soon rewarded. Lawrence leaned in and whispered, "He threatened to kill my mother and me if I published his name. After I pleaded with Mr. Turnbull, he reluctantly agreed to drop the story."

"I understand," Basil said. "I promise to keep your name out of this case. Can you tell me what you know about him?"

Lawrence huffed. "It's your funeral."

"I'll make a note of that."

"Very well. They call him The Griffin?"

"What? Like the . . . the bird?"

"Like the mythical creature, yer know? The one with the body of a lion and the head of an eagle? It's a symbol of the king of the beasts mixed with the king of the birds."

"Why do they call him that?" Basil asked.

"In ancient mythology, the beast was thought to be the guardian of golden treasure. It was also known for the power of the lion and the unassailability of the eagle."

Basil took a moment to absorb that.

Lawrence leaned forward again and lowered his voice. "What do you think happens when you trespass on a lion's territory or try to steal the egg from an eagle's nest?"

Basil narrowed his eyes at the challenge but said nothing.

"Look," Lawrence said, backing off. "Off the record again, just man to man, I'd run for the hills if I were you. Drop this case. Find another one to spend your time on."

As Basil got to his feet, Lawrence returned to his typewriter and his chicken-pecking.

"Thank you for your time, Mr. Lawrence."

Without looking up, Lawrence said, "Don't mention it."

Basil considered the newsman's warning. He'd thrown down a gauntlet, but instead of scaring Basil off, it made him more determined than ever to bring this Sharp man down.

15

*T*he next day, after breakfasting, Ginger waved off her American relatives as they continued with their London tour adventures.

"Are you sure you don't want to come with us?" Louisa asked, tapping her temple, missing the jewelled hair pin that kept her fringe from falling in her eyes. "You're spending too much time in here. We can do a little shopping. I'd planned to bring several new dresses home."

"I've more than enough gowns and dresses," Ginger said. "Don't forget I own a dress shop."

Sally adjusted the silk scarf tied neatly around her neck. "We'll have to buy another trunk."

Louisa grabbed Cornelius' arm. "We should go to Paris! We've come all this way. I can't bear to go back to Boston without an article of Parisian fashion!"

Cornelius smiled crookedly. "If you ladies want to shop, I'd be happy to wait in one of those public houses."

"You lot go and have fun," Ginger said. She had to hold herself back from physically pushing them along the marble floor of the entrance hall and out the front entrance. "The taxicab Pippins rang is waiting."

Breathing in the quiet once the taxicab motored away, Ginger ran through her usual routines—feeding Rosa and taking her for a walk in the pram, visiting Felicia and helping her pick out wallpaper for the dining room, and keeping up with the post, which included writing another letter to Scout. All the while, the case brewed at the back of her mind.

She and Basil had failed at tracking down Cecil Lawrence, but he wasn't the only newspaperman in town. Ginger snapped her fingers, mentally chastising herself for not thinking of Blake Brown sooner.

With Rosa in Nanny Green's safe hands, and Boss curled up in his bed by the fireplace in her study, Ginger picked up the black cradle telephone on her desk and dialled the operator. "*The Daily News*, please."

Once connected, she asked for Blake Brown and was pleased to have caught him at his desk. She and Mr. Brown had crossed paths occasionally, usually where a dead body was concerned.

"Blake Brown, here."

"Hello, Mr. Brown. This is Mrs. Reed. You'll remember me as Lady Gold."

"Ah, yes, of course. Lady Gold!"

Ginger pictured the man—serious with small brown eyes and receding hairline; she could almost see him move a short pencil, marred with teeth marks, and tuck it behind his ear. The tone of his voice was light, and she imagined him smiling as he continued, "To what do I owe the pleasure?"

"I'm working on a case, unofficially, and wondered if you'd be willing to answer a few questions?"

"Ah, I see." The sound of his chair scuffing across the floor, most likely a result of taking his feet off his desk, carried through the telephone lines. "And what, may I ask, is in it for me?"

"A story," Ginger said. "A proper one."

"The kind I like. Go ahead, shoot."

"What do you know about Cecil Lawrence?"

"From the Agency? He's a weasel. Will scoop another man's story without a second thought. Why? Is he the story?"

Ginger heard the eagerness in Mr. Brown's voice, typical of the critical competition amongst newsmen.

"Not directly. Did you hear about the death of a man dining at the Savoy two days ago?"

"Yeah," Mr. Brown said carefully. "Are you about to tell me that was foul play?"

"I'm afraid so. Mr. Reed and I were there as the victim's guests. Mr. Lawrence was there also."

"Do you think Cecil killed him?" Mr. Brown's voice was tinged with excitement. "You must promise not to give this lead to anyone else!"

"Mr. Brown," Ginger said sharply. "I didn't ring you to accuse Mr. Lawrence of anything, especially without evidence."

Basil had told her about the business fraud and the man Percy Aspen had testified against. She jumped ahead to her next question. "What can you tell me about Mortimer Sharp?"

"Changing the subject, are we?" He paused, and Ginger could hear him munching on his pencil. "Gangster fellow. Went up on business fraud charges. In the dashed clink since 1916. All respectable newsmen wanted to cover that story if they could, and if not, they most certainly followed it. Now let me ask you a question."

It was only fair, and she expected it. "Yes?"

"What's the name of the dead guy?"

"Percy Aspen."

Mr. Brown whistled. "You've got to be kidding. He's the bloke whose testimony finally put Sharp behind bars. Brave or stupid. Took off to South Africa or South America, I heard."

"Both," Ginger said. "He made some money in African mining and then headed to Peru."

"What brought him back to London?"

"I wish I knew."

"Well, I feel I've got the better deal here, Mrs. Reed. Do you have any other questions?"

"Hypothetically, if Mr. Lawrence killed Mr. Aspen, what would Mr. Lawrence's motive be?"

"Hypothetically? I have no idea. Honestly, I would've thought it'd be the other way around. Lawrence's cover of the story was watered down at best, and at worst, he made Sharp come off as a victim. Shoddy reporting on all fronts, and I'm not the only one to say it. He didn't work for a year after the trial, then well, there were other stories, and Lawrence can be good at his job if he wants to."

"Are you saying Mr. Lawrence's reporting was biased?"

"Yes."

"And that would've put doubt in Mr. Aspen's testimony."

"Indeed. That makes me think Aspen would've wanted Lawrence's head. Not the other way around. So, when are you going to tell me how Aspen died?"

"Poison."

"Poison? Blah. That's a lady's way to get rid of a problem. Though, Lawrence isn't a big guy. He might go for that. Look, I'll do some digging around and get back to you."

"I'd appreciate it," Ginger said, then gave him her house phone number.

She hung up the telephone receiver with a rattle, causing Boss to lift his head in question.

"More dead ends, Bossy." Sighing, she added, "Now what?"

As if in answer to her question, the telephone rang. "Oh, that couldn't be Mr. Brown ringing with news already, could it?"

It wasn't. Instead, she heard Basil's voice on the line.

"Darling, I'm heading to the Savoy."

"Oh? To see Mr. Aspen's room?"

"Yes. I'm heading there now and thought you might like to join me. Perhaps we can grab lunch afterwards."

"I most certainly will meet you." She took a few moments to tell Basil about her conversation with Blake Brown.

"Rather insightful of you to ring him, but I expect no less. His take on Cecil Lawrence's reporting is spot on. I remember it being a point of grief at the Yard at the time." He lowered his voice. "Morris is marching down the corridor. I'll meet you there."

Ginger grinned and jumped to her feet. Superintendent Morris would have a fit if he knew Basil was inviting her in on his case. But they did better when they investigated together, something the stubborn superintendent had witnessed often but wouldn't validate. As they say, two heads are better than one.

Boss barked as she flew out of the room. "Sorry, Bossy, you can't come this time."

16

"*Y*ou've only been on this for a day, Inspector." Morris struck a match and held it over the bowl of a briarwood pipe. Once the tobacco caught, he took a few puffs to stoke it whilst he waved the match in the air to extinguish it.

The whole action seemed to Basil to be one of detachment, a subconscious movement that revealed the man's casual indifference to Basil's postulations.

The chief inspector continued, "I doubt you've taken enough time to get something concrete to go on."

Basil would swear he could tell the man he'd just got a signed confession from Jack the Ripper and he'd sit there smoking his blasted pipe, barely sparing the time of day.

"Perhaps you're right, sir," Basil returned generously. "But why not give me a moment to explain what I have found so far. It might be worth talking about."

Morris huffed. "It doesn't have to do with that long firm scheme you mentioned, the one in Liverpool, does it?"

"Well, yes, I . . ." Basil stopped short when he noticed Morris rolling his eyes. "Really, sir, you should hear me out."

"Liverpool is a long way from London, and that was some time ago . . ."

"But there is a link."

Morris took another puff on his pipe and gestured for Basil to continue. "All right then, go ahead."

The room took on the smell of rich tobacco. Basil usually didn't like to smoke on the job. He preferred to savour the moment when he indulged rather than have it as an addendum to his work activity, but he had to admit: the tobacco smelled good.

"I interviewed one of the most well known and respected business owners here in London," Basil said. "One of the complainants from the list you gave me, by the name of Roland Wilcox. He told me the story of what happened to him, how he lost money to a fraud scheme, and it had exactly all the characteristics of the long firm ruse. There were others besides him who suffered a similar fate."

Morris waved his pipe in the air. "The long firm tactic?"

"Yes. Wilcox claims a certain name is common to every case: Mortimer Sharp, a man with gangster ties."

Morris shrugged a thick shoulder. "Doesn't ring a bell."

"It wouldn't, sir. Sharp has never been investigated in London, but he's our link to the crimes in Liverpool."

"And how do you know that?"

"I interviewed a reporter yesterday, a Mr. Cecil Lawrence. He's from Liverpool and was one of the reporters to write the story about the long firm frauds there."

"He reported on this Mortimer Sharp fellow?"

"Not explicitly. The reporters never published his name."

"Why the deuce not?"

"Because apparently, Sharp doesn't work alone. And according to this reporter, the fellow is known to be particularly vicious and keeps company with thugs who are not afraid to maim or kill. If they published names, the reporters were under threat for their very lives."

"Why would this gangster come to London if he was doing so well committing crimes in Liverpool?"

"The article Lawrence wrote resulted in the Liverpool police embarking on a campaign to stop these sorts of frauds. They couldn't pin anything on Sharp, but other arrests were made. This made it much harder for Mr. Sharp to pull off his fraud schemes."

The chief inspector seemed to absorb this as he puffed again on his pipe and shifted his considerable bulk on his chair.

"The thing is . . ." continued Basil, "Lawrence also told me that Mr. Sharp, also known as The Griffin—"

"The what?"

"The Griffin. It's a mythical beast, part lion and part eagle. The Greeks imagined it was the guardian of great treasures and would kill to protect them."

"Ridiculous." Morris deposited his pipe on an ashtray. "Some people certainly have a flair for the dramatic. "

"Nonetheless, this man was not just involved in long firm frauds, he was also known for racketeering and leading gambling rings . . . horse racing, and the like. A real bad character."

"Well, even if all this is true," Morris said confidently, "the man is no doubt fighting in France right now. Conscription was introduced in January, as you know."

"And as you know, Chief Inspector, there are ways around that."

"Yes, but it's not easy. And even if he did manage to escape military service, it would be hard for him to continue his criminal activities with any kind of real effect. Every able-bodied criminal is either in jail or in a trench somewhere fighting the Boche!"

"Be that as it may," Basil pressed, "he should still be tracked down and made to pay for his crimes."

"Yes, yes, yes, I know that," Morris returned irritably. "I was the one who handed you the case file."

"Yes, sir."

"Well, Inspector, I have my doubts. The whole thing sounds like a cheap detective novel. My advice is to do more digging. My guess is that some other pattern shall emerge, something a little less theatrical."

"Of course, sir," Basil said.

Just then, a postal courier appeared at the door.

"Special delivery for Inspector Reed," the man said. "I understand he is here?"

"Yes, that's me." Basil accepted the envelope and gave it a good look. It had no return address.

"Special delivery, eh?" Morris said. "Must be important."

"Curious, indeed," Basil said as he opened the envelope.

Inside was a short, typed note. After reading it, he handed it to Morris, whose face instantly drained of colour.

I've been told you are looking for me. I look forward to the chase, but if I were you, I would sleep with the lights on and hold the one you love closely.

I have many names, none of which you will be able to use in your dangerous quest, I'm afraid.

Just remember I am very territorial, and I have a nasty side.

So close and yet so far.

The Griffin.

*G*inger walked through the lobby of the Savoy, shoulders back and chin up, as she approached her husband. Basil took her hands, kissed her cheek, and then whispered, "If only we were checking in instead of snooping about."

"Next time, love," Ginger said with a tease. "Next time." Gazing around, she added, "Rather a nice place, but I expect Percy had grown accustomed to the comforts his newfound wealth had brought him."

Basil nodded. "When I first met him, he certainly came from humbler circumstances. Braxton is here and has obtained a key."

Ginger noted the young, uniformed constable standing to the side and offered him a smile in greeting. "Hello, Constable."

"Hello there, Mrs. Reed."

"How is Millie?" Millie worked for Ginger as a mannequin at her dress shop, Feathers & Flair. She and the constable had met during a previous case.

"She's terrific, Mrs. Reed. Thanks for asking."

The three of them headed for the lift, and Basil continued, "As soon as Percy died, I sent a man around to ensure the room remained untouched until I instructed otherwise."

As they stepped into the lift, the attendant asked for the floor number and closed the brass cage doors. Poor Constable Braxton grabbed the wall as the contraption jerked before moving up on grinding gears, a look of distress on his face.

Once they reached their floor and the doors were pushed open, Constable Braxton stepped into the corridor with a look of relief on his face before producing a key. As they stepped into Percy's hotel room, they were greeted with a waft of stale air.

"I see the maid hasn't been in either," Ginger said, flapping her gloved hand near her nose.

Basil opened a window. "I doubt a little fresh air will upset matters."

"What are we looking for, sir?" Constable Braxton asked.

"Anything unusual and out of the ordinary," Basil returned. "Financial papers would be grand."

Constable Braxton searched the water closet as

Ginger and Basil went through the chest of drawers and desk.

"No sign of female occupancy," Ginger said as she studied the wardrobe. "Nothing feminine on top of the furniture either. Not even a forgotten scarf or glove."

"Perhaps Miss Burton wasn't as close to Aspen as she likes to portray," Basil said. "For all we know, her presence at the Savoy was contrived by her."

"She might've presumed an understanding, much like Miss Chapman had in the past," Ginger said. "I've learned that men and women send signals to one another which are often misinterpreted."

Basil laughed. "We had a few of those ourselves early on."

Constable Braxton returned from the bathroom. "Nothing of note there. Men's shaving utensils and a towel on the floor."

"Nothing denoting a feminine presence?" Ginger asked. Had Miss Burton spent more time there than she'd let on? If Mr. Aspen had hinted that he wasn't inclined to propose, she might have felt an advantage had been taken.

Constable Braxton shook his head. "No, madam."

"Thank you, Constable," Basil said. "Mrs. Reed and I can take it from here. I'll meet up with you at the Yard."

The constable took his leave, and Ginger and Basil continued their search.

"Aha," Basil said. "His accounting notebook." He flipped through the pages.

Ginger stared with interest. "Anything?"

With a shrug, Basil said, "Our friend was worth a pretty penny, but I don't see anything unusual. At least he hasn't recorded any large amounts going in or out. No repetitive payments made to unnamed recipients."

"I suppose we can assume Percy wasn't being blackmailed," Ginger said. "But why had he gathered this particular group together? He had to have had a reason."

"Certainly not for old times' sake," Basil said. "None of us, apart from your family, had anything in common that we would care to reminisce about."

Ginger's attention was taken by a stack of envelopes pushed to the back of a drawer. Hidden correspondence usually revealed scandalous or nefarious goings-on. She opened the top envelope and read the note inside.

"Basil?"

Basil looked up from Percy's financial papers. "Love?"

"I've found something."

Basil stepped in beside her and she handed him the

slip of paper. Staring at the lines of sharp, left-leaning cursive, he scowled.

"Threatening letters," Ginger said.

Basil pursed his lips. "I don't know how it's possible, but I think I know who the author of these letters is."

"Do tell."

"A fellow named Mortimer Sharp."

"From the case Mr. Aspen testified at?"

"Yes. It must be the reason he gathered us together at the Savoy," Basil said. "Besides you and your family and Miss Burton, the rest of us were involved with the Sharp case, one way or another."

"I'm surprised he included your family in the invitation," Ginger said.

Basil cocked his head. "Quite likely, he originally meant for me to bring you, not all your relatives."

"Oh yes," Ginger said. "I do recall Percy looking a mite perturbed."

"It didn't stop the killer from going through with his plan," Basil said.

"Or her plan," Ginger amended. "Where is Mr. Sharp now?"

"He's still in prison," Basil said. "We need to learn how he found Percy and how he managed to get these letters to him."

18

*S*ince Basil had returned to the Yard to follow up on the status of Mortimer Sharp, Ginger decided to drive back to Hartigan House to check on little Rosa. However, at Trafalgar Square, she saw the familiar figure of a young man lumber by.

"Marvin?"

Locking her eyes on the young man, she missed seeing a motorbus slowing to a stop and swerved to miss running into it at the last minute. She hit a kerb instead and landed with one tyre on the pavement. Ginger didn't bother to right her motorcar but jumped out instead to chase down the lad. Marvin Elliot was Scout's older cousin, who, as far as Ginger knew, was engaged with theRoyal Navy. It had been that or prison, so seeing him meandering about the streets of

London, dressed as a civilian in dirty, worn-out clothes was deeply alarming.

"Marvin!"

The young man swivelled to her voice, his eyes bugging wide as recognition hit. Ginger had played a big hand in helping the cousins, first giving Scout extra "jobs" on the SS *Rosa* as a ruse to give him an extra shilling or two. Later, she did so again when they were reacquainted in London, where the two lived in squalor with an ailing uncle.

Marvin had been tempted into a life of crime, nearly killing Ginger in the process. It had landed the lad in prison and Scout in Ginger's care as her ward. She'd pulled strings to get Marvin off easy, so long as he served king and country as a sailor, so overall, she thought he owed her an explanation or at least to show signs of being pleased to see her.

Instead, he pivoted and ran like a shot.

"Marvin!"

Ginger broke into a light run, in so much as her two-inch heels would allow. She was good at many things, but sprinting wasn't one of them. Marvin was younger, faster, and soon lost in the crowd.

Oh mercy. What had the lad got himself into now?

Checking her wristwatch for the time, Ginger sighed. Little Rosa needed her attention, so she couldn't very well be driving around London, searching for a young man, amongst many young men, all dressed the same in various shades of brown.

To Ginger's dismay, the American faction had returned and taken over the sitting room. It wasn't Louisa or Sally that had her hackles up, but that blasted, pig-headed Cornelius. Ginger hoped against hope that Louisa would come to her senses and give the cad the boot.

Hearing her enter, Louisa stood at the double doors that opened into the sitting room and waved her over. "Ginger, you must join us. We had such fun at the Tower Bridge! Mama almost fell into the Thames!"

It would have been rude of Ginger not to spare a few moments. She handed her coat and hat to Pippins, thanking him, then joined her family.

"I could've drowned," Sally said with a huff.

"Good thing I was there to save you," Cornelius said.

Sally shot the man a firm look. "You're the reason I almost fell in!" To Ginger, she explained, "He acted like he owned the bridge, bouldering through the tourists. Knocked me with his elbow into the railing."

Louisa laughed. "It was an accident, Mama. Cornie would never hurt you on purpose."

Lizzie came in with a pot of coffee, a second offering, Ginger saw, and put the carafe on the table.

"Would you like milk, sir?" Lizzie said with a slight bend of the knees.

"Yes, I want milk," Cornelius said. "Do I constantly have to repeat myself here?"

"No, sir," Lizzie said.

Ginger noted the glint of defiance in her eye and wondered what else, besides milk, she was pouring into Cornelius' coffee. Whatever it was, it would likely have him making several trips to the loo, and the rude oaf deserved it.

At least Louisa frowned in her fiancé's direction. Ginger's half-sister was used to privilege, but she was never purposely harsh with the staff.

Cornelius resumed reading a London newspaper he'd placed to the side, a week old, Ginger noted, but presumably the man didn't care or didn't notice.

He guffawed. "Your country changed its name, I see. It's now Great Britain and Northern Ireland. What happened to the south?"

"The Irish Free State is no longer part of the United Kingdom."

Cornelius slapped his thigh. "Hot dog! Revolt against the royalists! My kind of folk."

Ginger rose to her feet, not wanting to get into the intricacies of Irish relations with someone who knew absolutely nothing about it. "I must see to my daughter."

. . .

Ginger loved her American family, but even without Mr. Gastrell, she found her half-sister and stepmother took up a lot of space. With Mr. Gastrell, Ginger found it hard to breathe, so once Rosa was tucked in the cradle for her afternoon nap, Ginger slipped outside and sneaked around the back of the cul-de-sac to the back entrance of Felicia's house.

The maid gave Ginger entrance. With a curtsey, she said, "Lady Davenport-Witt is in the drawing room."

"Thank you," Ginger said. "I'll find my own way."

The former Whitmore residence, now the secondary Davenport-Witt residence, had been a tired-looking place before Felicia moved in. The drawing room had been dreary and suffocating. Ginger and Felicia had found great delight in tearing down the dark and heavy drapery, and with fresh rose-coloured paint and lighter mint-green curtains, the room was already much more inviting. Felicia wanted to wallpaper one wall but was having apparent difficulty in making a choice. She glanced towards the opened door when she heard the heels of Ginger's T-strap shoes clicking on the tile floor.

"Ginger! What a marvellous surprise." Felicia held

up a wallpaper sample. "Roses? Or is it too feminine? Charles thinks I should go with geometric shapes."

"Geometric shapes are very fashionable," Ginger said.

"You're right. I'll go with geometric shapes. Now what colour? Black or white, rose and green?"

"Let me close my eyes," Ginger said as she let her eyelids fall. "Mix them about, and I'll make a random choice."

After the sound of shuffling, Felicia said, "Ready."

"The one on the right."

"The black and white," Felicia said. "Yes, I think it's perfect. And Charles will be pleased."

Ginger lowered herself into an armchair—a new arrival. "I'm so happy to be helpful!"

Felicia rang a bell for the maid then took the matching armchair. The maid arrived in good time, bending at the knees and curtsied. "My lady?"

"Tea for two, please."

The maid dipped at the knees. "Right away, my lady."

"I'm a little surprised to see you," Felicia said. "Aren't you rather occupied with the Americans?"

"Rather," Ginger returned. "I love them, well, two of them, but they can be a handful. I'm here for a bit of respite. How is Charles, by the by?"

"He's dandy. I'm expecting him soon. You can ask him yourself then."

The maid returned with a tea tray, setting it on a small table between Ginger and Felicia. Felicia poured and handed the teacup and saucer to Ginger, who accepted it carefully.

Felicia sipped her tea then asked, "Anything new to report on poor Mr. Aspen? I'm still stunned that our dinner at the Savoy turned out so tragically."

Ginger had hoped her former sister-in-law would bring up the case. Before marrying Charles, Felicia had often helped Ginger out at Lady Gold Investigations and had developed a keen investigative sense of her own.

"It's all rather convoluted," Ginger said. "Though we did get confirmation from Dr. Gupta that Mr. Aspen had been poisoned."

Felicia's grey eyes flashed with interest. "Poison? What kind of poison?"

"A rather obscure one called Lucineride." Ginger filled Felicia in on the characteristics.

"It had to have been administered by someone seated next to him," Felicia surmised. "I was to his right. It must've been Miss Burton!"

Ginger tapped her cheek with a long finger. "Unless it was administered before we sat down. Mr.

Aspen had coffee whilst the rest of us enjoyed champagne."

Felicia huffed. "Oh dear. It could've been anyone."

"The suspect list is a mite long," Ginger agreed.

"And how did the person know the lights would go out? It's an oddity that couldn't have been planned ahead."

Ginger tilted her head. "Couldn't it?"

Felicia worked her lips. "Well, if one did count on the lights to go out, one would need someone working on the inside, wouldn't one?"

"Perhaps, but the Savoy's fickle electrical system's problem is well reported in the newspapers," Ginger said. "For now, let's assume that the killer was in arm's reach and hoped the lights would go out as expected, planning to strike when it did.

"Have you or Basil spoken to anyone yet?" Felicia asked.

"We've spoken to Miss Burton. She appears to be a gold-digger, so an alive Percy Aspen would be more beneficial to her than a dead one."

"Unless Mr. Aspen was hesitant to set a date for the wedding," Felicia said. "Many men like a pretty young thing on their arm and never, as they say, mean to make honest women out of them."

"I dislike that colloquialism," Ginger said, "but a spurned woman can indeed be dangerous. There's a mystery lady connected with her story, a Miss Mary Jones. According to Miss Burton, Miss Jones arranged for her to encounter Mr. Aspen as they travelled by ship from Brazil."

"What about Mr. Lawrence?"

"The newspaperman is proving elusive, but I've rung Mr. Brown to see if he could offer anything helpful from the inside."

"And?"

"He clearly dislikes Cecil Lawrence. Interestingly, Mr. Lawrence reported on the trial of a gangster called Mortimer Sharp, and not very well, according to Mr. Brown. The same trial Mr. Aspen had testified at."

"Ohh," Felicia hummed. "The plot thickens."

"Which reminds me," Ginger said, leaning in. "How's your book coming along? *Murder on the Rhine*, isn't it?"

In recent years, Felicia had made a name for herself as a mystery writer. Not with her own name but using the nom de plume Frank Gold.

"That's the title currently," Felicia returned with a pout. "I'm at a tricky point in the plot where I need to figure out how the little boy could hide in the old grandfather clock without the mechanisms stopping. My editor is expecting pages soon, so I really need to solve this quickly I thought picking out wallpaper would allow my subconscious to work on it in the background." She smiled. "But this is better! Now, what about Mr. Yardley?"

Ginger shook her head. "He was very uncooperative. He must have something to hide, but your guess is as good as mine at this point. He's a banker, so hopefully, it'll come up as the Yard studies Mr. Aspen's finances."

Felicia stared out of the window, her eyes blank.

"What is it?" Ginger asked.

"It's probably nothing," Felicia returned. "In fact, I'm sure it's not."

"But . . ."

"Well, at the end of the evening at the Savoy, I overheard Cornelius tell Louisa that he'd met Percy Aspen before. Apparently, he'd been on an expedition in Peru, and Mr. Aspen was part of the team."

Ginger's jaw grew slack. "How interesting that he never mentioned as much."

"He can't be involved with Mr. Aspen's death," Felicia said, then added, "Can he?"

Ginger recalled the seating arrangement at the Savoy. Cornelius Gastrell wasn't within arm's reach. Was it possible that he'd worked together with another? Why hadn't he divulged this information? She pinched her lips together as she got to her feet. "I'm afraid I will have to endure another awkward conversation with Mr. Gastrell."

asil left the offices at Scotland Yard in a very troubled mood. He had only just begun his investigation and had already identified the main culprit in a series of dastardly business frauds. But his quarry had already realised he was being pursued and seemed to look forward to it. That The Griffin had got this information so quickly was very disconcerting, to say the least, as was the boldness of the action itself. Roland Wilcox and Cecil Lawrence were the only people outside Scotland Yard's upper ranks who knew about the investigation.

But what about Mortimer Sharp? Who were his allies? How had he and his gang—for surely a group of men were needed to pull off these crimes—evaded conscription? Was he currently involved in criminal activity, or was he merely hiding from the military, writing his letter to Scotland Yard by candlelight in some rented room in an obscure corner of London? What kind of man invites, even dares, the police to go after him anyway?

Basil mused as he walked briskly towards the nearest underground station. Jack the Ripper had allegedly sent a letter to London's Central News Agency in 1888, the famous "Dear Boss" letter, taunting the police and causing a sensation in the headlines. However, that letter was thought by many to be inauthentic and written by one of the journalists to garner more subscriptions to the newspaper.

The Griffin's missive wasn't sent to the press and was directed at Basil. Whoever he was, the intention was personal and not for gain of notoriety. This alone made it more likely to be authentic.

Basil's jaw muscles clenched. He wouldn't rest until this Griffin man was brought to justice.

He spent most of the day visiting each business on the list that Roland Wilcox had given him. Besides Roland Wilcox, there was a steel manufacturer, a textile importer, a supplier of suspension parts for motorcars, and a leather merchant. All the businesses were successful, the owners captains of commerce in their own right, even during these trying times. And every one of them told similar stories about the man they were convinced had swindled them.

According to the description the business owners gave Basil, Mortimer Sharp was a man in his thirties, tall and slim, with a high forehead and slicked-back sand-coloured hair. His eyes were described as brown and beady, and he wore no moustache or beard. The textile importer described him as someone with a formidable presence who carried himself with great confidence. The leather manufacturer, an excitable man, described him as resembling an eagle, with a long, hooked nose and hooded eyes that seemed to know more about you than they should.

Whoever he was, The Griffin seemed to be one who left an impression on people.

Hopefully, Basil thought as he dodged a horse and carriage, his pride would prove to be the unscrupulous man's downfall.

20

This new, intriguing, and potentially dangerous information about Louisa's new fiancé had Ginger's mind spinning. What did her half-sister really know about this man?

Cornelius was obviously a man of means—or at least he did a fine job of pretending. Ginger could imagine him pompously parading through jungles with a revolver at the ready, believing himself to be an expert huntsman. The loud timbre of his voice along with his heavy-footed gait was enough to frighten any prey into hiding.

Ginger marched into Hartigan House to search every room, if necessary, to insist that Cornelius give an account of his silence at the Savoy when she practically ran into the wall of his body as he exited at that exact moment.

"Ginger, sweetheart!" he said with a glint in his eye, his hand clasping her shoulder a moment longer than necessary. "I wish I could have this dance . . ." he laughed, and Ginger pulled away.

"You're about to take your constitutional?" Ginger asked.

Cornelius' ruddy cheeks grew redder. "That's a personal matter, isn't it? Besides," he chuckled again, "I'm aware of the restroom at the end of the hall."

"Constitutional, in this sense, means a walk."

"Huh? Well, why didn't you just say that? You British have to sound so . . ." he waved a hand by his nose, "snooty."

"I'm sorry if I've offended you, Cornelius," Ginger said. "It wasn't my intention at all. I feel we've got off on the wrong foot. Would you mind if I joined you? We must learn to be friendly if you're to become part of the family."

Cornelius relented with a superior huff, his expression clear that he was doing her a favour.

"I suppose. You can tell me about the neighbours."

As they strolled together side by side around the perimeter of Mallowan Court, Ginger regaled Cornelius about the widow Mrs. Schofield and the tempestuous friendship she had with Ambrosia, and about her memories as a child playing with the neighbours' children. As they rounded back, Ginger pointed to the residence across the court.

"Charles and Felicia—Lord and Lady Davenport-Witt—live there. Lord and Lady Whitmore once owned it."

"Lord and Lady! You Brits and your stuffy titles. I'm not about to call anyone my lord or my lady, that's for sure. It's plain old Mr. and Mrs. to me."

"Well, yes, I concur that the fine point of British polite address may be a trifle difficult to comprehend for foreigners like yourself."

Cornelius shot her a confused look as if he were uncertain whether he'd been slighted or not.

"Actually," Ginger started before the fellow developed a headache trying to figure it out, "I'm pleased to have a moment to chat. I've learned something interesting, and I wonder if you could make sense of it."

Cornelius puffed out his chest. "I'd be delighted to help a little lady such as yourself."

"Splendid. Tell me, how did you like the excursion to Peru?"

Cornelius gave her a quick sideways glance. "Who told you that?"

"More to the point," Ginger said with a tilt of her chin, "why didn't you tell me?"

A quickened gait followed a shrug. "No one's business but my own."

"Except that you were part of the same group Mr. Aspen was in."

"Coincidence."

"Coincidences in a murder investigation are fascinating to the police."

Cornelius stopped, his nostrils flaring. "It's true, Aspen and I had a run-in. Accused me of undermining his authority. Hogwash! Not my fault the man couldn't read the map in front of his face. If it weren't for me, our group would've walked off a waterfall!" He sniffed in an effort to regain his composure. "It was so long ago, he didn't even recognise me. Not worth mentioning."

"Did you know Mr. Aspen was coming to London?" Ginger pressed. "Was that why you came to London?"

"No, no, no. I told you. Coincidence. Nothing more."

"Did you know of Basil's connection with Mr. Aspen?"

"What connection?"

"The trial of Mr. Sharp, a known gangster. Basil was a lead investigator and Mr. Aspen a prime witness."

Cornelius puckered his lips as he slowly shook his head. "Nope."

Ginger considered the belligerent man. He was precisely the type to discover Louisa's connection with

Mr. Aspen through herself and thus Basil, and pursue her with a ruse of romantic promise, just to find an old nemesis, if Mr. Aspen was indeed one.

"Well, coincidences do happen." She forced a smile. "Shall we turn back?"

With a grunt, Ginger's future brother-in-law pivoted on a heel and started back with a vengeance, forcing Ginger to skip along to keep up. After a few minutes, she gave up. There was nothing one could do if a man refused to be a gentleman.

GINGER TOOK her time returning to Hartigan House. Settling her emotions whilst walking around the garden to the back, she admired the daffodils. A while later, as she meant to head upstairs, she found Ambrosia at the base of the staircase, gripping the railing with bejewelled fingers.

"You've just missed them," Ambrosia said with a note of exasperation.

Ginger didn't need to guess who the dowager meant by "them".

"Ten minutes in their company, and I need a lie down," Ambrosia continued,

"They do seem to come with their own weather system," Ginger said. "Did they say where they've gone?"

"Out for dinner somewhere." Her cheek twitched slyly. "Mrs. Beasley barely contained her pleasure when Mrs. Hartigan relayed the news."

Ambrosia continued her hike up the staircase, and Ginger kept pace. "I had a rather uncomfortable chat with Mr. Gastrell," Ginger confessed. "I'm worried for Louisa."

Ambrosia gave Ginger her standard round-eyed look. "Had you heard the row they just exposed the rest of us to, you wouldn't be as worried. That young Louisa is brighter than she appears. Don't be surprised if Mr. Gastrell is given his marching orders before too long."

Ginger appreciated that Ambrosia could see through her half-sister's flightiness. In time, Louisa would grow out of her "bright-young-thing" phase. No one stayed young forever. She hoped Ambrosia was right about Louisa catching on before it was too late.

Leaving Ambrosia at her bedroom doorway, Ginger headed for the nursery. Rosa, gurgling on Nanny Green's lap, brought a big smile to Ginger's face. "Rosa!"

Nanny lifted the child and handed her to Ginger. Ginger brought the soft bundle to her face and kissed her daughter on the head. "Hello, sweetie. Did we have a nice nap?"

"She did, madam," Nanny said. "And half a bottle of milk since."

After playing with Rosa, Ginger returned her daughter to the nanny.

"I'll care for her until she's tucked in, madam," Nanny said. "Then I'm meeting my sister. The nursemaid is staying overnight."

"Very good," Ginger said. She was so pleased with Nanny's proficiency that she'd make any allowance the nanny wanted to keep her happy. Not that she had any concern that Nanny was looking for work elsewhere. Ginger paid her very fair wages, and the attachment growing between Nanny and her daughter was obvious.

Ginger wanted to speak to the head waiter at the Savoy before the evening rush and had enough time to visit the Savoy before dinner. At the hotel, she relinquished the keys of her Crossley to a bright-eyed valet.

"Lovely machine, madam," he said.

"Thank you," Ginger returned. She thought so too.

Inside the lobby, Ginger sought the concierge. "I'm looking for the head waiter in charge of the Aspen party two nights ago. Evans, I believe."

"Oh, yes, madam. That was a dreadful affair. I'm afraid it rather shook Evans up."

Ginger tensed. Did that mean the waiter wasn't on

the premises? What bad luck to have to track him down in the city.

The concierge continued, relieving her of her consternation. "The manager has got him writing out work schedules until his nerves settle."

"He's on the premises?" Ginger asked hopefully.

"Yes, madam."

"I'd love to speak to him, if possible." She glanced about the posh lobby. "Somewhere below stairs, perhaps?"

The concierge nodded. "Please follow me."

After traipsing through a maze of corridors, the concierge stopped. "Please wait here, madam."

The sounds of pots and pans banging and cooks shouting reached her as the concierge pushed through a door. Moments later, Evans, now wearing his black waiter's uniform, appeared before her.

"Oh, good afternoon, Mrs. Reed."

"You remember me," Ginger said. "How delightful."

"It's pretty difficult to forget anyone from that night."

Evans' memory was what Ginger was counting on.

"I agree. As I imagine is true for you, I've been reliving the events of that night repeatedly, and I just know if I can make sense of it, I may be able to push it out of my mind and get a decent night's sleep. Wouldn't you like that too?"

Evans nodded weakly. "Yes, madam."

"Fabulous. Perhaps we can help each other."

"I'm not sure how, madam. I don't know anything."

"Oh, well, sometimes our minds work behind the scenes, so to speak, and something that seems irrelevant and forgettable suddenly becomes the most important point."

"All right," Evans said, not sounding sure at all.

"Did you ever meet anyone who was part of the Aspen party before that night? Perhaps at another event or restaurant?"

Evans shook his head. "No, madam." He offered a soft smile. "I've heard of you, of course, from the rags, and Lord and Lady Davenport-Witt, but it was my privilege to meet you for the first time here at the Savoy."

"Apart from my family members, did anyone approach you separately, perhaps to ask a favour?"

Evans swallowed. "The lights, madam."

"I beg your pardon? What about the lights?"

"A messenger boy came with a note. It said if I flickered the lights, there be a few bob in it for me. The note assured me it was merely a prank to be played on a friend." Evans' gaze fell to the floor. "Look, my family comes from humble means, and every quid helps. I'm lucky to have this job." He glanced back at Ginger with imploring eyes. "Please, don't say anything."

"Your secret is safe with me," Ginger said. "Now, was the note signed at all? Do you know if it came from a man or a woman?"

"No, madam."

"When did you receive the note?"

"Just before your group arrived, madam."

Ginger considered the timing. The note came before she and her family arrived, but after the others had already been seated. It was possible that someone from that small group, Miss Burton, Mr. Lawrence, or Mr. Yardley, could've arranged for a note to be served during that short while.

There was also the latecomer, Miss Chapman.

"Thank you, Evans," Ginger said, slipping a shilling into the waiter's hand. "We can keep this conversation between ourselves. I'm certain we'll both sleep better now."

"Thank you, madam," Evans said enthusiastically before disappearing back into the kitchen.

Ginger checked the time and sighed. Mrs. Beasley liked a timely dinner hour. Ginger would have to save her desired visit to Miss Chapman until the morning.

21

A name that came up often during the interviews with the businessmen was Percival Aspen, an independent accountant who did the books for at least some of The Griffin's fake companies. After some digging, Basil discovered that Mr. Aspen now worked for an accountancy firm in central London, having abandoned his own business. After enquiring at the reception on the ground floor of a tall brick building, Basil took the stairs to the top floor, occupied in full by the sprawling offices of Smythe and Biggins. Another receptionist, a pleasant man named John David, greeted Basil and then disappeared down the corridor. Basil heard him announce his presence, followed by a moment of silence, likely attributed to the surprise of suddenly being visited by a Scotland Yard Inspector.

The young man reappeared and led him back down the hall to the office of Percival Aspen.

Despite a clear redundancy, Basil introduced himself. "Inspector Reed from Scotland Yard, Mr. Aspen. I hope you don't mind answering a few questions."

Mr. Aspen's eyes, large behind thick lenses, flashed with a concern that a long, hard swallow failed to eradicate.

"My, this is curious," Aspen said. "We don't have much occasion for members of the police force visiting here." After shaking Basil's hand, he gestured to a leather chair directly in front of his desk.

Basil took the chair as Aspen settled back into his, now with a willing smile and a demeanour of cooperation. "What can I do for you, Inspector?"

If Percy Aspen had any criminal involvement, he would try to hide it. Sometimes, a sudden and direct approach was best to probe a subject's inner thoughts. When confronted with something unexpected, one could tell quite a bit from someone's body movement and facial expression.

"I'm hoping you can help provide information on a man I'm looking for."

The accountant exhaled as if relieved that he wasn't the subject of Basil's probe. "Yes?"

"Mortimer Sharp, otherwise known as The Griffin."

Aspen's smile instantly faded, his face draining of colour. He huffed, left his seat, made strides towards the door. Basil wondered if the man was about to walk out on him, but thankfully, he only meant to close the door.

"I guess it was only a matter of time," Aspen said. He blew air out of a pursed mouth as he lowered himself once again onto his chair.

Basil took out his notebook from his breast pocket. "Tell me what you know."

After a tired-sounding exhale, Aspen said, "Mr. Sharp's a savvy businessman; that was his reputation. At first, I was honoured to be sought out by him to keep the books for several businesses he'd recently acquired. I was new and working on my own, which . . ." Aspen ran a slender hand across his face, "which was exactly the attributes he was looking for." Aspen locked eyes with Basil. "Imagine the lamb being separated from the flock as the wolf plots the animal's demise."

Basil thought the analogy rather dramatic, but he nodded his support. He waited Aspen out, and the man soon jumped in to fill the silence.

"Let's just say it didn't take long for me to realise that Sharp was expecting me to do things that I found . . ." Aspen worked his lips, appearing to struggle to find the right word. His eyes turned upwards as he released another sigh.

"I can't do it," he said finally. "He would kill me.

He told me he would, and I know he would carry through with that threat."

"I understand, Mr. Aspen," Basil said gently, "but withholding this kind of information is against the law."

Aspen held Basil's gaze challengingly. "Someone would have to prove that in court, which would be impossible."

Hoping to appeal to the man's conscience, Basil leaned forward as he said, "This man needs to be stopped." After a pause, he added, "I'm willing to do my part."

Aspen clasped his hands tightly. "I don't think you understand the gravity of the situation. These are violent men. And Mortimer Sharp does not make idle threats. We all die sometime, Inspector." Aspen stared at his hands. "But I consider it a worthy goal in life not to die a violent and premature death."

Basil considered the accountant for a moment. The man's testimony would be integral should this case get to trial, but he was balking at the prospect of testifying, much like all the other business owners had. Roland Wilcox had been the exception, but Basil didn't know if his lone testimony would be enough.

What kind of hold did this Griffin fellow have on people?

"What if I got you police protection?" Basil said, not

knowing if he could convince Morris to agree to the expense.

"What?"

"Police protection. We can place officers on watch around the clock until Sharp is locked away in prison and we are sure his allies are either apprehended or fighting in France."

Aspen nervously ran his fingers through his hair and shook his head slowly. "I don't know, Inspector."

"Are you married?" Basil asked. "Parents? Family?"

"My parents have passed away, and I have no siblings."

"Then it's simple! We would form an impenetrable wall around you. You would be helping to put an evil man behind bars, Mr. Aspen."

Percy Aspen leaned forward, put both elbows on the desk, and buried his head in his palms.

"By all that's holy, I'm just a pencil pusher." He pointed to his spectacles. "Even the military doesn't want me. I'm not a deuced hero or intrepid figure in someone's adventure novel. I work with numbers." He picked up a pen and then dropped it again on the desk as if to underscore his point.

"And yet you have the ability to put a very powerful, evil man behind bars with just a few sentences spoken in front of a judge," Basil said. "That makes you one formidable pencil pusher indeed."

22

*G*inger was delighted to discover that Ambrosia had invited Felicia and Charles to join them for dinner. It'd been a while since the two couples had spent time together without Louisa and her gang in the midst. Mrs. Beasley had prepared a delicious fish pie.

"Grandmama," Felicia said, addressing Ambrosia. "You simply must come and see what I've done at Davenport House."

Ambrosia stifled a shiver. "A new name can't undo old memories."

It had been known to those on Mallowan Court as the Whitmore House, and although Ambrosia and Lady Whitmore hadn't seen eye to eye, Ginger thought the dowager was making a bit too much of it. Ginger suspected Ambrosia's contempt was directed more at

Felicia's choosing to be mistress of the old Whitmore residence over the grand Witt House on Wilton Crescent in Belgravia.

"Oh, Grandmother," Ginger said. "You won't even recognise the place. It's like the Whitmores have never lived there. And besides, you can't refuse to visit your own granddaughter on occasion."

Ambrosia looked down her nose, and blinked her slow, round-eyed blink. Her fingers went to her hair, which had grown in recent months, and she had got her maid Langley to pin it up again, just like Ambrosia used to wear it in the Victorian times. Cutting her hair was one of Ambrosia's great regrets.

"Very well," she said, tapping her walking stick on the floor. "The distance is not so great that I can't make the journey."

Felicia flashed Ginger a grateful grin that Ginger returned, acknowledging a shared victory.

Once they finished eating, Ambrosia excused herself, ringing for Langley to help her to her room whilst the two couples retired for brandy in the sitting room.

Giving the newlyweds the settee where they could sit closely by design, Ginger took one of the armchairs situated close to the tall windows, pulled her shoes off, pushed them to the side, then rested her feet on the ottoman. Boss, having followed them into the room, panted happily when Ginger patted her lap, the leap taking some effort with his short legs. A fire had been lit in the stone hearth, and her eyes breezed over the Waterhouse painting of a red-headed mermaid.

Basil headed to the side table, uncapped the glass decanter, and poured four glasses, two fingers-full each. After delivering the drinks and taking the second armchair, he said, "Charles, how are things at the House of Lords?"

"Fairly uneventful," Charles returned. "But you, old chap, you're the one with the interesting job. How is it with your case? So dreadful what happened to your chum Aspen."

"My investigation is dredging up an older case," Basil said. "At first, I didn't think the two could be related, but it's starting to look like they might be."

"Oh?" Felicia said.

Ginger noted the glint of mystery-solving curiosity in her grey eyes. "How so?"

"Eleven years ago, Mr. Aspen testified at the trial of a man involved in several business fraud schemes."

"Was this man present at the Savoy?" Charles asked.

Basil crossed his legs. "Not at all. In fact, he's still in prison."

"I don't understand," Felicia said. "How could this man be involved?"

Ginger noticed the slight twitch in Basil's jaw. He respected Felicia's work as a mystery writer but hadn't got to the place where he trusted her judgement in a real case. On the other hand, Ginger had seen Felicia in action and had no problem including her in the discussion.

"That's exactly what we're trying to figure out, Felicia," Basil said. "The interesting thing is that three of Mr. Aspen's guests were also connected with that old trial."

"You don't say," Charles murmured. "What was the bloke's name who broke the law?"

After a sip, Basil replied, "Mortimer Sharp."

"Ah," Charles said.

Basil took note. "Does the name mean anything to you?"

"Only that I remember the case. We got London papers in France." He glanced towards Ginger for a split second; she and Charles were the only ones in the room who understood the significance of that statement, as they both, though not together, had worked secretly for the government. "The news didn't mean much to us on the battlefield, except we felt some contempt for the Sharp fellow for not doing his bit in the trenches."

"It turned out that Sharp didn't have a legitimate

reason to stay in England either," Basil said. "Another fraudulent event."

"And you investigated this Mr. Sharp?" Felicia asked.

"It was his first case as a new inspector," Ginger answered proudly.

Basil loosened his tie, glancing away bashfully, a move Ginger found adorable.

"Felicia told me something interesting, love, about the night at the Savoy," she said.

Basil raised his chin. "Oh?"

"You mean Mr. Gastrell?" Felicia offered. "Yes, well, as we were leaving, I heard him mention to Louisa that he had met Mr. Aspen before, and when she asked where, he told her on an expedition in Peru." She patted Charles on the arm. "Darling, did you hear that?"

Charles shook his head, looking disturbed. "I must've had my attention drawn elsewhere. You're sure that's what he said."

"She's right," Ginger said. She could imagine what Charles was thinking. He was the one trained to watch and listen. Missing this credible clue would irk him. "I spoke to Cornelius myself."

Basil locked his hazel-eyed gaze on her. "Do tell."

"He was rather unpleasant," she started.

Felicia snorted. "Nothing new there."

"Yes," Ginger agreed, "but he did admit to knowing Mr. Aspen from an expedition they were both on."

"Did he know Aspen would be in London at this time?" Basil asked.

"He says no. Everything is a "coincidence", by his accounting."

Basil huffed, then finished the last sip of his brandy. "I should like to speak to the man myself."

"Can you imagine?" Felicia said, her cheeks rosy from the effects of the brandy. "Mr. Aspen's attacker a guest in our home? What a scandal! Grandmama would never leave the house again."

Ginger scrubbed Boss behind the ears, rousing him. "We mustn't jump to conclusions. We don't even know how the killer administered the poison. Cornelius would need a very long reach to have tainted Mr. Aspen's food during a short blackout. Unless . . ."

Basil raised a brow. "Yes?"

"Unless the poison was dropped into Mr. Aspen's coffee before we even sat down to eat."

Felicia nodded in agreement. "We were all mingling."

"Gastrell would only have had to distract Aspen for a moment," Basil added.

"With the poor chap's bad eyesight," Charles said, "especially in that low light, it's possible."

As Ginger rubbed Boss' back, she said, "I took the

opportunity to call in at the Savoy to speak to the head waiter."

Basil cocked his head. "My, you've been busy."

Ginger simply shrugged. "I'm sure one of your men has been around already," she said, though Evans never indicated that he'd been questioned.

"What did you discover?" Basil asked.

"A note came to him by messenger boy, offering to pay if the waiter made the lights go out for a good while. He thought a prank was about to be played."

"Some prank," Charles said.

Felicia snorted. "Quite a convoluted mystery."

"Perhaps I can be of some assistance," Charles said. "I have contacts at the House of Lords. Someone may know something about this Sharp fiend or the guests of Percy Aspen that might shed some light."

Afterwards, as Ginger and Basil got ready for bed, Basil said that he doubted Charles could be of much help.

But Ginger knew better. When Charles spoke of the House of Lords, he meant a circle much wider, if not quieter, than that.

23

The next morning, Louisa informed Ginger that she, Cornelius, and Sally were going to take a day off from playing the tourist. "Cornelius is under the weather," she said. "It's just a cold, but the slightest ailment turns him into a big baby." A yawn escaped her rosebud lips. "I'm tired out too. Vacationing can be exhausting!"

"I'll be out and about," Ginger said. "There are plenty of books in the library, if you care to read. Enjoy a restful day."

After feeding Rosa, Ginger wrote to Scout and gently asked if he'd heard anything more from Marvin. She then left Hartigan House with hopes of visiting Winifred Chapman. The April sun shone through sycamore trees filling out with vibrant green, pointy leaves as the sparrows twittered—sure signs that spring had come to London, even if one had to experience it through wisps of fog and blackish plumes of petrol belching from the back of busy motorcars.

Ginger, parking her Crossley rather askew, headed inside the building where Winifred Chapman's flat was located, Boss happily following on his leash.

"I can't help but think that Miss Chapman is the key to this mystery, Bossy," she said through lips shiny with pink lipstick. She'd been told that pink clashed with her red hair, which was precisely why she liked to wear it. Besides, only the tips of her bob were visible under her felt cloche hat, nicely decorated with felt daisies and petunias, suitable for the season.

After her knock on the door was unanswered, Ginger called out, "Miss Chapman?" She'd be satisfied with either Miss Winifred or Vera.

She knocked again. "Miss Chapman?"

Clearly, both Miss Chapmans were out. Ginger glanced at Boss, who watched her with round brown eyes. "What do you think?"

Ginger's thoughts were on the set of lock picks. Not a typical accessory found in a lady's handbag, but Ginger wasn't a typical lady.

Ginger removed a glove and slipped her fingers into her bag, fingering the ring of picks, but before she could retrieve them, the door next to the Miss Chapmans opened.

A white-haired lady, still wearing her dressing gown, squinted at Ginger. "Who's is it?"

"Hello," Ginger said warmly. "I'm Mrs. Reed. I'm looking for Miss Winifred or Miss Vera Chapman. It appears you are neighbours. Have you seen them lately?"

The lady lifted a shoulder. "Who?"

"Your neighbours. Miss Winifred is the elder, about thirty-five, and her niece is in her twenties."

"Only seen them a couple of times. Mostly the younger one."

"Thank you, Mrs . . ."

"Cooper. Mrs. Cooper."

"Thank you, Mrs. Cooper. I'll call again later."

Ginger made a show of heading to the staircase, Boss on her heels. Mrs. Cooper disappeared behind her door, and when Ginger heard the lock click, she stepped quietly back to the Chapman residence, her lock picks at the ready.

Boss, used to his owner's shenanigans, waited silently. The wagging of his stubby tail indicated his anticipation. Ginger listened for the pins to drop, and the door swung open.

"You wait by the door, Bossy, and alert me to any noise you hear on the stairs."

Boss settled on his black haunches, taking his assignment seriously, his nose sniffing the air.

Ginger made a quick cursory look around the flat to ensure that the tenants were indeed out and found it the case.

Not only that, to Ginger's dismay, the flat looked unoccupied. Though it had never looked like it had been made into a home, there had been signs of persons dwelling in it: coats hung by the door, gloves on the side table. A jaunt into the bedroom confirmed that no clothing or personal items were to be found. Curiously, there was only a narrow bed fit for one. Ginger wondered where the niece had slept. The living room settee, perhaps, though it was short and narrow and not suitable for sound sleeping.

Where had the Chapman ladies gone? And more importantly, why? Ginger's interview with Winifred Chapman had only happened the day before last, and she hadn't indicated that she was preparing to move away or leave London.

The timing was terribly suspicious.

Boss whined, and Ginger tiptoed to the door. She could see a man enter through the railing, heading up the stairs. She stepped out of the Chapman flat, closing the door before he reached the top. She scooped Boss into her arms and passed him in the corridor. He tipped his hat, "Good day, madam."

"Good day," Ginger said, her mind already on her next move—a trip to Scotland Yard.

24

*B*asil stared blankly at the file opened on his desk. He'd worked at Scotland Yard on the Victoria Embankment for many years, first as a constable, sergeant, then an inspector, and now as a chief inspector. He recalled his first day on the premises, shortly after he was released from the hospital and declared fit for "light" work, and how awed he was by the impressive-looking Victorian buildings made handsome with red brick and bands of white Portland stone. At the time, he'd thought he'd only stay for as long as the war lasted, but before too long, he realised that investigating was in his blood. He enjoyed the puzzle, the chase, and ultimately, if things went his way, seeing justice take place.

He dreamt about his cases at night, awakened eagerly in the mornings to get back to it, and since

Ginger had come into his life, recalled his best moments again in front of the fireplace in the sitting room of Hartigan House over a glass of brandy.

Life was good. And now, with Scout and little Rosa in the mix, it was very good.

But this case—he tapped a finger on the page facing him—was different. It caused him to circle back to his first case on the job as an inspector at the Yard, a case, though he clearly remembered it, he rarely thought about. A plethora of cases had opened and closed in the meantime, and always the most current case was at the top of his mind.

Percival Aspen had fled in fear for his life. Why had he come back to London? And why had he called this particular group of people together?

Or was it purely happenstance?

Basil had a hard time believing that.

Besides, Mortimer Sharp was still in prison. Basil had rung the prison administration and confirmed it for himself.

However, Sharp had a long reach. One of his hooligans could be responsible, but how? Who in the room could've killed on his behalf? Basil had followed up on the staff, interviewing that Evans waiter again, and even done a police background check on him and members of his family. No one was guilty of anything beyond not paying their tab at a pub.

It just didn't make sense.

He perked up at the sound of a female voice. The owner was cheerful and inviting like a bubbling brook, greeting the constables as she confidently strolled by. Basil had to bite his cheek when she stepped into the doorway of his office, so elegant, even with Boss in her arms.

Lordy, he loved that woman!

"Ginger," he said, reining in all his base emotions that just wanted to grab her and lock the door. "Always a pleasure."

His wife sashayed to the empty chair and sat down. The office, when Ginger was absent, was more than efficient for his needs. A simple wooden desk and office chair, a couple of ladder-back chairs for visitors, and a stack of filing cabinets, but with Ginger in the room, everything became even more drab and understated. She never mentioned the decor, or lack of it, for as much as she was highly fashionable and an admirer of beautiful things, she was practical. At first blush, one could be forgiven for underestimating his wife—her joie de vivre and youthful demeanour often disguised her incredible intelligence. But Ginger was a keen observer and master puzzler. Basil had learned early on that he must never underestimate her.

"I've just come from Winifred Chapman's flat,"

Ginger said, plucking her gloves off one finger at a time.

"What did she have to say today?" Basil asked.

"I couldn't tell you, love. She wasn't there. Neither was her niece. In fact, it appears they have vacated the place."

Basil raised a brow. "And how would you know that, my dear? Don't tell me you've learned to see through doors."

Ginger laughed. "Would you be surprised if I said I have?"

"Not at all, actually. Let's just move on from the question of how. Could you ascertain where they have gone?"

"No. But interestingly, it appeared that only one person slept in the bed."

"Perhaps the niece slept on the settee."

"I thought that too, but it doesn't look like anyone sat on it, much less slept on it. Not a cushion out of place, not a lost crumb. However, she may've been the tidy sort who leaves a place cleaner when she leaves than when she arrived."

Basil furrowed his brow in thought. "Frightfully unusual, especially after a 'dear friend' has died. I'll put Braxton on it. See what he can come up with for Miss Winifred Chapman and her niece."

"Vera," Ginger said, filling the blank. "Also, there's this."

With the dog in her arms, Basil failed to see the folded newspaper she had tucked there too. Ginger folded it out on Basil's desk.

"What am I looking for?" Basil asked.

"Cecil Lawrence's story on Aspen's sudden death at the Savoy, and all the juicy bits about Kaspar the Cat and superstition."

Basil frowned at the paper as he scanned the headlines. He flipped to under the fold, then through the pages.

"I don't see it."

"That's because it isn't there," Ginger said. "It hasn't been in any of the news headlines since it happened. Don't you find that odd? I recall that Mr. Lawrence was rather keen to scoop the story, and yet . . . no scoop."

THIS TIME, when Basil and Ginger visited the London News Agency, Cecil Lawrence was conveniently seated at his desk. When the newsman spotted them, he shrunk into himself as if that would make him invisible. Basil shouted over the noise of the clicking typewriters and a loud talker using the telephone.

"Mr. Lawrence! Good to see you!" Adding for the sake of the room, "It's Chief Inspector Reed."

"I bloody well know who you are," Lawrence muttered. His eyes scanned Ginger in a way that made Basil want to sock the fellow on the nose. Lawrence wasn't the only one to notice Basil's wife. The buzz in the room dimmed as the men watched Ginger stroll across the pit. "Good day, fellas," she said with a wave of her free hand. The other held her dog, which Basil was certain wouldn't be allowed in the newsroom were it being carried by anyone else. People were often so taken by Ginger's dynamic personality, they were willing to overlook a small canine. Basil certainly had been when he first met Ginger on the SS *Rosa*, and he still was now.

Keeping his cool, he pulled a chair aside for his wife, and she accepted it with a flourish. "Thank you, love."

Basil was captivated by Ginger's bright green eyes, creamy skin, and fine figure. Still, he only let his gaze linger for a moment, reminding himself that he was operating in a professional capacity. He snapped his fingers to remind the room of the same, and the noise of typewriters and chatter returned to the normal decibels.

"I'm a busy man," Lawrence said with a grimace. "Get to it."

"I'm waiting for your scoop," Basil said. "You know, Mr. Aspen's untimely and sensational death?"

Lawrence sniffed, relit a half-smoked cigarette he rescued from an overflowing ashtray, then propped his feet on the desk. "I was assigned to something else. It happens."

"Mr. Lawrence!" Ginger said with a slight tilt of her pretty head. "You were quite keen to write it. Rapturous, even."

"Yeah, well, things happen."

Basil used a glove to flick away the smoke of Lawrence's next exhale. "You know what I think? I think you got scared off." He locked his eyes on Lawrence and, with a verbal twist of a knife, added, "again."

Lawrence's feet dropped to the ground. "Poppycock!"

"I think you're afraid of Mortimer Sharp," Basil said. "He scared you into writing a fluff piece on him when he went to trial, and he's scaring you now with Aspen's death."

"Bwaa. You're making things up now, Chief Inspector."

Basil pushed, "How did he get to you? Bribes? Blackmail?"

"Threatening letters?" Ginger added. "Our poor Mr. Aspen was a victim of those."

Lawrence's jaw slackened, and if it weren't for his sticky lips, his nearly finished cigarette would've fallen from his mouth. "Look, I'm just a bloke trying to do my job and pay my bills." He crushed what was left of his cigarette and added it to the pile on the ashtray. "Like any of this lot."

Basil kept pressing. "Did the threats come by letter or messenger?" When Lawrence failed to respond, he added, "Mr. Lawrence, I'll remind you that this is a murder investigation. Your lack of cooperation could suggest culpability."

Lawrence snorted. "On what evidence?"

"That someone present in the Savoy dining room poisoned Percy Aspen, including you."

"I recommend you do a bit of digging on Yardley," Lawrence said.

Basil took the bait. "What do you think I'll find?"

"That he's got somethin' against Aspen."

"Like what?" Basil asked impatiently. "Deliver the goods and get on with it."

"Before Aspen scuttled off to Africa, he went to Yardley for a loan." Lawrence sniffed, then continued. "Aspen didn't have two farthings to rub together at the time. Yardley had to pull strings, even fudge on lending rules, to get the cash."

"Seems good of the chap," Basil said.

"Yeah, well, Yardley got the sharp end of the stick

when Aspen defaulted on the initial payments. Aspen was so afraid of the bogeyman, he used that fear to convince Yardley that blood would be on his hands if he didn't hand over the dough."

"Turns out Mr. Aspen had reason to be afraid," Ginger said.

Lawrence shrugged, then removed a cigarette from a case he pulled from his shirt pocket and lit up again. "Correlation doesn't necessarily mean causation, Mrs. Reed. Yardley put his neck on the line and lost the bet. He happened to be up for a promotion at the time, but when the bigwigs found out what he had done, they reprimanded him and demoted him. He was humiliated." Lawrence blew smoke over his shoulder. "A bloke doesn't get over that kind of thing."

Basil caught Ginger's eye and offered a soft shrug. Lawrence had a point. If he was telling the truth. He'd get Braxton to follow up on the story.

25

*A*fter checking in at the Yard the following day, Basil headed to Dagenham and back to Roland Wilcox's factory. Like the last time Basil had called, the place was full of activity. He wondered how people could take the nonstop noise day in and day out, as he bristled with agitation after mere minutes.

When he got to the top of the iron stairway, he knocked hard on the office door. After a minute of no response, Basil stepped down the wrought-iron gangway and peered in the window. The room appeared empty; no one was seated at the desk. Turning around, he scanned the floor below for signs of the burly factory owner. A man wearing a leather apron and hat looked up at Basil and waved in acknowledgement. Basil climbed back down to greet the man.

"Jake Telford." The worker shouted to be heard as he offered his hand to Basil. "Factory foreman."

"Ah, very good. I'm Inspector Basil Reed from Scotland Yard. Is Mr. Wilcox on the premises?"

Telford shook his head, then said, "Come with me."

Basil followed the short man into a small, dirty office, which quieted adequately when the door was shut.

"Blasted noise out there," Telford said with a huff. "A man can't even 'ear 'imself think."

"I'm looking for Mr. Wilcox."

"Yeah, you and me both, Inspector. 'E's not come into work yet."

"Oh?" Basil was surprised. "Does Mr. Wilcox frequently come to work late?"

"Well . . ." the man cleared his throat. "Not recently. 'E stopped drinkin' a few months ago, but lately . . ." Telford shrugged. "'E's back in 'is cups."

"I see," Basil said. "Does he have a favourite drinking hole?"

"The Old Bell and 'Ound. I've joined 'im there on occasion, but I leave when I get the feelin' I might 'ave to carry 'im 'ome, if you know what I mean. They do serve a good shepherd's pie, though." The man's hand went involuntarily to his stomach. "There's no shortage of workin' blokes there for Wilcox to drink with on most nights."

Basil glanced at his watch. It was still mid-morning. "Where does Wilcox live?"

"Barking."

"It is a matter of some urgency," Basil said, thinking for a moment. "I could go through Barking on my way back to Scotland Yard."

"Yes, you could try 'im at 'ome. I'm sure 'e's gathered 'is wits by now."

Half an hour later, Basil was again knocking on a door, waiting for a response from within. When Wilcox failed to respond, Basil leaned into the glass window and cupped his hand on the glass to shield it from the sun's reflection. Inside, he could make out a kitchen with some dishes left unwashed, and beyond that, a sitting or living room. There seemed to be no one home.

Frustrated, Basil let out a long breath. Going back to the Yard with nothing of significance to report to Morris smarted.

He stepped back and gazed up at the red-brick building, and then, on a whim, he walked down the street and around to the back lane. A window of the ground-level flat had been smashed in, the hole large enough for someone to reach in and unlock the latch. The window was closed, but through it, Basil could see shattered glass all over the floor of a bedroom.

"Blast it," he said aloud as he stared at the window. "First week on the job . . ." Throwing caution to the wind and risking the ire of his superiors, he wrapped his hand in his handkerchief, reached in, and opened the window.

Inside was an unmade bed, and a small table with a ladder-back chair angled in the corner. On the floor in front of it, Roland Wilcox was lying in a pool of blood, his throat slit.

he next morning, Ginger and Basil took breakfast in their bedroom at the table in front of the tall windows. Nanny had brought Rosa in to join them, and Ginger took special pleasure in spending time with just the three of them.

Well, four, if you counted Boss, curled up into a black ball at the foot of the bed.

"Can we do this every morning until they leave?" Basil asked dryly. "They *are* leaving, aren't they?"

Ginger fed Rosa, who was strapped into a wooden baby seat. "Sally did mention needing to get back to the brownstone in Boston but failed to state a timeline. I wouldn't be surprised if Cornelius wasn't at Kensington Addison Road Station as we speak, buying a ticket to Liverpool to get out of the country."

"If he's guilty, he won't be going anywhere," Basil

said. "I've put a bulletin out to delay his departure until cleared by the Yard."

Ginger gasped. "Oh mercy. A blight on our family name, isn't it?"

"He's not family yet, love. And by grace from above, he'll never be."

Ginger held the same hope. Louisa made a good show of standing by her man, but Ginger knew her half-sister well, and those sharp looks she darted in Cornelius' direction were signs of a crack in the foundation of their relationship. Ginger always liked to give someone the benefit of the doubt, but Cornelius Gastrell wasn't the kind of man one wished on one's sister. In Ginger's opinion, Louisa could do much better.

They finished their breakfast of toast and tea, eggs and sausages—Ginger slipping a morsel to Boss, who'd positioned himself under the table—with little Rosa grabbing porridge from the spoon and dropping it on her head.

Basil laughed. "She's got more on her face and bib than in her mouth. I'm surprised she's as chubby as she is."

"Babies are meant to be chubby," Ginger said, feigning offence. "It's a sign that they're healthy."

Basil wiped his mouth with a cloth napkin. "I know that, love. I haven't had a chance to tell you, but

Braxton rang this morning, and Lawrence's story about Yardley turned out to be accurate."

"Interesting."

"Indeed. Are you staying here with Rosa, or do you want to join me to meet Yardley?

"Can I not do both?"

"I don't think that would be prudent."

Ginger pouted, but Basil was right. She couldn't very well push a pram into the bank and then question an employee regarding a motive for murder.

"Rosa is due for a morning nap," Ginger said. "She won't even miss me."

Basil smiled as he pushed away from the table. "I'll ring for the nanny and have her draw the baby a bath. Then I suggest you hand her over to Nanny and meet me out the back by the motorcar."

Later that morning, Ginger and Basil walked into the bank like a monied couple about to bring the bank good business. The branch manager, who hadn't been on the premises when they'd last visited Yardley, approached with hopeful appreciation flashing in his eyes and an extended hand. "Welcome to Barclays. How may I be of service?"

"We'd like to see Mr. Yardley please," Basil said.

The manager's mouth twitched in barely disguised disdain. "I'm certain Mr. Yardley would be pleased to assist you with your banking needs;

however, I'm equally capable, and it would be my great pleasure."

Ginger wanted to stop Basil before he stated that they were on police business. There was no need to bruise Mr. Yardley's reputation further if he was innocent of Mr. Aspen's murder.

"Mr. Yardley is a family friend," she said. "My aunt Dottie would be disappointed if we didn't speak to her favourite nephew."

"Very well," the manager said with a tone of surrender. "If you grant me a moment of your time, I'll fetch him."

Mr. Yardley's demeanour crumbled when he saw Ginger and Basil, clearly unhappy to see them again. He tugged on his waistcoat and, with stiff professionalism, said, "Chief Inspector Reed, Mrs. Reed, how may I help you with your banking needs today?"

"Mr. Yardley, my good man," Basil said cheerily, "a moment of your time, please. A little privacy would be appreciated by all."

Mr. Yardley led them to a consultation room, where the three seated themselves at a round table.

"Mr. Yardley," Basil began, "it's come to our attention that there was a bit of bad blood between you and Mr. Aspen."

With his knees jumping nervously under the table, Mr. Yardley said, "What has passed is past."

"He came out well," Ginger added, "but you paid for his good fortune, didn't you? If not for Mr. Aspen, you'd be the manager of this bank by now."

Mr. Yardley tightened his lips as if he could keep from spewing his true feelings by pure strength of will. "Like I said, what has passed is past."

Basil turned to Ginger and said, "Aspen did invite him to join us for dinner at the Savoy . . ."

Ginger played the game. "Forgiveness between friends is admirable . . ."

"But eleven years is a long time . . ."

"Betrayal is hard to truly forgive . . ."

"Think of how Mr. Yardley's life might've been . . ."

"Financial stability, social respect . . ."

"All gone . . ."

"Enough!" Yardley spat. "I let myself get sucked in by Aspen's despair, and I pitied him. I helped him. And did he remember me at all? Yes, he paid up finally, too late for me, but that didn't absolve him. When he invited me to the Savoy, I thought perhaps he meant to apologise."

"When you realised that wasn't his intention, you killed him," Basil said.

"No." Mr. Yardley let out a pathetic chuckle. "I wouldn't have been brave enough to do it, even if I wanted to." He looked to Basil, then Ginger, as if appealing. "Think as poorly of me as you will; I'm not a murderer. Did I wish that Aspen had lost his fortune? Certainly. That would've been poetic justice in my mind. I rather hoped that he'd brought us together to ask for money. A plea for support on a new adventure or some such nonsense. I'd planned a big speech to deny his request, lay out my grievances to everyone, and get my revenge in humiliating him as every friend he thought he had in London left him to cry in his soup." Mr. Yardley removed a handkerchief from his breast pocket and dabbed at his forehead. "I assure you, Chief Inspector Reed, Mrs. Reed, I didn't kill him."

"Thank you for your time," Basil said as they got to their feet. "Please don't leave town."

Outside, Ginger linked her arm with Basil's and said, "I'm leaning towards believing Mr. Yardley, as pathetic as his story is."

"Without a confession of guilt," Basil said, "we've nothing to hold against the man, and no evidence to prove otherwise."

The sound of a brass horn honking alerted them to the police motorcar that zoomed to the kerb, with Constable Braxton at the wheel. He jumped out to greet them. "Sir, madam. Front desk told me you had gone to the bank, sir."

"Braxton," Basil said, "what have you got?"

"News regarding Miss Chapman, sir. I thought you'd want to know right away."

Ginger stopped herself from impatiently tapping her T-strap shoes. "What is it, Constable?"

"She's dead."

Oh mercy.

"Where's the body?" Basil asked.

"That's the thing, sir. She died five years ago. She's buried at St. Mary's."

asil entered the Old Bell and Hound pub in Barking and made himself at home on a stool at the bar. He ordered a pint of Guinness and struck up a casual conversation with the landlord, a balding man in his early fifties with a tattoo the shape of an anchor on his left forearm.

"Not the busiest tonight," Basil said after taking his second sip and glancing around the room. A dozen people were seated at tables, leaving him solo at the bar.

"It'll pick up a bit." The landlord wiped the surface of the bar with a cloth that looked like it could use a cleaning. "Nothin' like it was before conscription, mind you."

Basil looked for any sign of irony or inference in the man's voice. After all, Basil was a seemingly fit and able-bodied man himself. He didn't sense any.

After a few minutes of polite banter, the landlord said, "Don't know if I've seen you in our establishment before."

"You haven't. I live in Mayfair."

The man whistled. "Posh. Well, you've wandered a bit far from 'ome, then."

Basil had always admired a landlord's skill at conversation, often drawing out information without even asking a question.

"Actually, I'm here on police business," Basil said, then added with a nod at his pint, "although perhaps more in an unofficial capacity, if you get my meaning."

"Ah, yes, I do." The landlord chuckled. "I'm always eager to 'elp. What can I 'elp you with, Officer?"

"Inspector . . ." Basil corrected, getting used to the sound of his new title.

The landlord cut in before Basil could properly introduce himself. "Righto. Inspector. I'm the owner of this 'ere establishment, and nothin' goes on 'ere without my knowin' it." He flipped a white towel over his shoulder then leaned an elbow on the bar.

"Do you know a man named Roland Wilcox?" Basil asked.

"Of course I do. 'E ain't done nothin' wrong 'as 'e?"

"No, but I understand he was here last night?"

"That's right. Same as always."

"I'm wondering if you might have noticed . . ."

The landlord suddenly snapped his fingers, leaned in, and lowered his voice. "You're Inspector Reed."

"That's right, I am," Basil said with a note of surprise. He looked around the room and motioned for the barman to keep his voice low. He didn't want his identity broadcast to the whole room.

The barman obliged, saying in a half whisper, "Wilcox mentioned you last night, several times. You're looking into the trouble 'e ran into last year."

"He talked to you about me?" Basil asked.

"No, not me. 'E was with another bloke, both sittin' 'ere at the bar. I 'eard 'im plain as day."

"Did anyone else hear him?"

The landlord pushed out his lower lip. "Beats me."

"What was Wilcox saying?"

"Only that Scotland Yard had finally sent a man over to 'is place to ask questions about what 'appened. 'E said you seemed like the type of bloke that would get the man who done it."

"Anything else?"

"Oh, 'ol Wilcox always says many things when 'e's 'ad a few, and 'e don't care who 'e says it to, neither. Yes, 'e said somethin' about a man who 'e thought was responsible. 'E said 'e was 'opin' you would do your snoopin' around that fella mostly."

"Did he mention a name?"

"Well, you would know the name, wouldn't yer?"

"Yes, but did he mention it?"

The landlord nodded. "'E said somethin', but it wasn't a name like a man's name, it was somethin' else like . . ." He snapped his fingers as if that would stir his memory. "Like a bird of some kind, but I can't remember."

"What do you know about the man he was talking to?"

"Nothin', really. "'E's only been 'ere a few times. Don't really know 'im."

Basil sighed. "Then I suppose you don't know where I can find him."

The landlord leaned in close and discreetly pointed to a man on the opposite end of the room who had just stood up to leave. As if he had an appointment he needed to keep, the man looked at the clock behind the bar as he pulled on his cap.

"Thank you, sir." Basil put money on the bar for his drink, adding a generous tip. "Please keep this conversation between us, if you don't mind."

The landlord scooped the coins off the bar's surface. "Mum's the word, Inspector."

Basil adjusted his trilby as he stepped out into the night air and onto the cobbled street, keeping a good distance between himself and the man he was following. The stranger, who walked with a pronounced limp, looked to be in his early thirties. He wore a grey, ill-fitting suit jacket and a brown cap. Basil expected him to make his way to Barking station two streets away. From there, one could catch the District Line and easily connect to anywhere in London. And indeed, the man headed straight for the station, but instead of entering, he walked north.

The man's gait was slow, and Basil guessed his leg injury came from time spent in France. This forced Basil to duck behind buildings and into alcoves to keep from view, especially since the man would often stop and look nervously around him.

Eventually, the man ducked into another pub called The Grey Horse. Chances were good that the man would be there for a while, at least as long as it took to down a pint. Basil searched the area for a bobby, and after trying a couple of streets, he found one swinging his truncheon.

Basil introduced himself, explaining to the constable what was happening. The constable followed Basil back to The Grey Horse.

"Are you familiar with this establishment?" Basil asked as they approached it.

"Yes, sir, it's my favourite pub, sir,"

"Is there a back door to the kitchen?"

"Yes, there is, and I know the cook very well." In his late twenties, the young constable was sharp and seemed to guess what Basil had in mind.

After the constable had disappeared around the side of the building, Basil took a deep breath and entered the pub. Though more crowded than the previous establishment, it still was only at half capacity. The man with the limp had taken a seat at the far end of the dimly lit bar, a drink in his hand. Basil claimed the stool at the opposite end, ordered another Guinness, and waited. He could only guess who the man was to meet, but he had a good idea.

Basil's hunch was rewarded when, moments later, a tall, slim man with a long nose and slicked-back, sand-coloured hair entered. Walking confidently, gliding along the floor, he matched the description the business owners had given Basil.

Basil pulled the brim of his trilby down low and took a long sip of his beer. He was reasonably confident that The Griffin didn't know what he looked like but couldn't know for sure.

Basil's heart beat a tick faster. The man with the limp had happened to be in the Old Bell and Hound when Basil had gone there. Basil had found the street constable within minutes, and now his quarry sat within reach. Luck seemed to be on his side.

After Basil had discovered Roland Wilcox's body, the police conducted the preliminary work, and a post-mortem was ordered. Perhaps fingerprints would be found, or some other telltale sign. No matter. With the testimony of Percy Aspen, Basil had what he needed to arrest the man they called The Griffin. If he could also convince the business owners to testify, Mortimer Sharp would go to prison for business fraud. Then, once Basil could gather enough evidence to link him to the murder of Roland Wilcox, The Griffin would hang. Basil considered following The Griffin home and then gathering a few men from Scotland Yard for the arrest, but he didn't want to risk losing the man now that he was so close within his grasp.

After a deep breath, Basil crossed the room and eased himself onto the stool next to The Griffin, who gazed back at him through the reflection in the mirror that hung crookedly on the wall behind the bar.

"There's the rest of this bar where a thirsty man can have a beer," Mortimer Sharp said, locking eyes with Basil's reflection. His voice was smooth, but it carried more than a hint of menace.

"I like this spot just fine," Basil said. "It'll serve well for what happens next."

The man's eyes narrowed as he spun to look at Basil face-to-face.

"Mortimer Sharp?" Basil said as he calmly reached into his side pocket with his right hand and gripped the cold steel of a set of handcuffs. Basil had noted that both of the man's hands lay palms down on the bar.

"Who wants to know?"

Basil stood as he slipped the ratcheted handcuff onto the startled man's right hand in one quick motion. The Griffin instantly tried to resist, which Basil was hoping for. With a quick and practised move, Basil pulled the right arm back and up sharply whilst pushing the man's head down with his left hand. That forced The Griffin's shoulder and head onto the bar, knocking over and spilling beer. Brown liquid spread across the surface and dripped onto the floor. Basil then moved his left hand over to grab the left hand of the man bowed over the bar and forced it back and up to slip the other manacle on.

"What? How dare you!" The Griffin shouted, his words muffled due to his face being flattened on the bar. The attention of everyone in the room was now on them. Having secured the man's hands, Basil leaned his elbow onto the crook of The Griffin's back, forcing him to stay with his cheek pressed against the bar.

"Mortimer Sharp, you are under arrest!"

The man with a limp dashed, as fast as one with a bum leg could, to the back door, only to be stopped by the constable, his truncheon at the ready. "Steady now," the constable said in a low but firm voice. "One move from you and my set of shiny handcuffs shall nicely fit your wrists too."

28

*G*inger and Basil sat in the Austin, staring straight ahead at nothing.

"If Winifred Chapman is dead," Basil started, "then who was the woman at the Savoy?"

"Our killer," Ginger said. "A clever ruse."

Basil lifted his chin. "You said she had a niece."

"A woman who claimed to be a niece. Come to think of it, I never saw the two Chapman ladies in the same room simultaneously." Ginger mentally chastised herself for not noting that fact at the time. It signalled a loss of the sharp mental edge she'd honed in France, granted, a life and death situation had a way of putting one on constant alert. "Ten to one, the woman is long gone now." Basil had sent his constable over to investigate. Ginger continued, "I doubt Constable Braxton will find anyone there."

"You could be right," Basil said.

"I'd like to know who Mary Jones is."

"Mary Jones mentioned by Helen Burton?"

"Yes," Ginger said. "It's curious that this Miss Jones seemed to go out of her way to introduce Miss Burton to Mr. Aspen. Miss Burton thought it was a kindness on the stranger's part, but perhaps Miss Jones had a nefarious motive."

"Such as?"

"She may have found it easier to watch Mr. Aspen under the guise of Miss Burton's friend." Ginger tapped a lacquered fingernail on her lips. "If she's the author of the threatening letters—perhaps her hand-writing is similar to Mortimer Sharp's with left-leaning cursive—Miss Burton's friendship might've given her access to Mr. Aspen's stateroom, a way to deliver them anonymously."

Basil started his Austin and, after checking over his shoulder, pulled in front of a bright red double-decker motorbus.

"Off to see Miss Burton?" Ginger asked.

"Yes," Basil said, speeding precariously through a junction. He glanced at Ginger. "I'm starting to drive like you."

Ginger lifted her chin. "I have no idea what you mean."

At Miss Burton's flat, Basil knocked, and after a

long wait, Ginger feared they might have another disappearance. Clearly, Miss Burton and the woman impersonating Miss Chapman couldn't be the same, but they could've worked together to murder Percy Aspen.

Just as Basil was about to bang the knocker again, the door opened, Miss Burton staring back wearily from the other side. "Yes?"

"Miss Burton, might we come in?" Basil asked.

Miss Burton's shoulders slumped as she sighed. "I hardly have a choice, do I?"

"All the same," Basil said as he crossed the threshold, "it's polite for one to ask."

Ginger followed Basil, stepping aside as he closed the door. "We won't keep you, Miss Burton," she said. "We only want to ask you about Miss Jones."

Miss Burton's demeanour brightened. "Oh, all right. I'm not sure what I can tell you beyond what I've already mentioned but ask me your question."

Ginger shared a look with Basil as it was clear Miss Burton had no intention of inviting them inside any further than the entry. Either way, the interview would proceed.

"Do you recall ever meeting Miss Jones before the time on the steamship?" Basil asked. "Perhaps in Brazil? That was where you were coming from?"

"Yes, as I said before, I was on holiday there, and

on my way home when I met Miss Jones and Percy. I don't recall seeing Miss Jones previously."

"Did you find it unusual for her to seek you out for friendship?" Ginger asked. "Did she travel in first class with you?"

"Yes. At least she claimed to."

"Didn't you wonder why this Miss Jones didn't seek to set herself up with Mr. Aspen?" Ginger asked. "He was a very eligible bachelor."

Miss Burton fussed with the lace handkerchief in her hand. "I did wonder that, actually, but Miss Jones seemed distinctly uninterested. She did little to present herself. Never fussed with her hair or her clothes. Never wore a touch of make-up."

"What did Miss Jones look like?" Ginger asked. "Close up."

"Short nose dotted with freckles. Light eyes, neither blue nor green. Straight, mousy-brown hair. She could've been pretty if she made an effort, but as I said, she seemed to prefer being overlooked."

Ginger turned to Basil. "She's described Vera Chapman."

hree days later, Basil boarded the underground line to Vine Street Police Station in Westminster. The last few days had been quite heady for Basil. The relatively quick arrest of a suspected racketeer who might even be a murderer brought many congratulatory remarks from within the corridors of Scotland Yard. Even Chief Superintendent Knowles had unexpectedly dropped in with a bottle of ten-year-old single malt Scotch. Basil had enjoyed a slow and smooth glass of it that very evening.

Mostly due to the war, and even more so since the new conscription law, London had been relatively free of significant crimes for a time. The arrest of someone like Mortimer Sharp seemed to have served as a morale booster for Scotland Yard; the police force wasn't just a bunch of scallywags sitting around on their thumbs and evading the war.

Granted, it was a bit of a dampener to walk into Morris' office the day after the arrest. Basil had expected a positive acknowledgement, but all he got was a reminder that the suspect had not yet been found guilty in front of a judge and that Basil still had a lot of work to do to bring about that result.

Despite that, Basil felt chipper in his second week on the job as he entered the station and checked in with the reception desk.

Ten in the morning. He was right on time.

A few minutes later, he sat at a table in the interrogation room, facing Mortimer Sharp.

The composite description that the complainants had put together for Basil was accurate. The man really did exude a sullen confidence that put one in mind of an eagle in repose. His hooded, dark brown eyes regarded Basil as if he were a curiosity, something to examine first before he decided whether to devour it or not.

Remarkable, given that he was the prisoner and Basil the inquisitor.

The Griffin wore prison clothes, but his hair was still immaculately slicked back. He leaned away from the table with his manacled hands resting lightly on his lap and his legs crossed.

"*Cigarette?*" *Basil tipped an open package of Craven A towards the prisoner. He didn't often take to smoking, but felt it was a way to portray a kind of calm, in-control demeanour when questioning a suspect who couldn't or wouldn't indulge.*

Basil noticed a twinkle of amusement pass across the man's eyes.

"*No, thank you.*"

"*All right then,*" *Basil said as he sat back and exhaled a plume of smoke from the side of his mouth. He nonchalantly tossed the pack of cigarettes onto the table.*

"*Inspector Basil Reed,*" *Mortimer Sharp said, the corners of his mouth turning up into a smile that Basil could only describe as sly. "You must be feeling quite pleased with yourself. New on the job, I hear, and already bagged your man, eh?*"

How did he know that Basil was newly ranked as Inspector? Basil forced himself not to show any expression of surprise.

"*I only have you to thank for that,*" *Basil said. "It was kind of you to send me that letter, really.*"

"*Oh?*"

"*Yes. I just followed the trail it left. You made the mistake of letting me know that you knew I was on your trail. In other words, I just looked for the leak. Someone had to have told someone.*"

The Griffin narrowed his eyes. "Yes, well, I tend to

agitate my enemies unnecessarily." He inhaled slowly through his teeth. "I love being dramatic."

"I suggest losing that habit quickly," Basil said, "considering where you're going."

The Griffin chuckled softly, a strange, dry sound, like two dusty bricks rubbing together. "I'm not as sure as you are, Inspector, about my prospects of extended incarceration."

"Let's talk about that anyway, shall we? My advice is to be very forthcoming about your activities here in London. That way, you might yet see the natural light of day before you're an old man. Judges are always more lenient on the repentant."

"Whatever do you mean? I'm a law-abiding citizen in every sense." The Griffin turned his palms upward and shrugged his shoulders in an expression of mock incredulity.

"Unless, of course, you murdered Roland Wilcox. You would hang for that."

The prisoner stared at Basil for a moment, his expression blank. He blinked once, slowly, reminding Basil of a barn owl.

"Who?" The Griffin said as if reading Basil's mind.

"The honest man you bilked out of a lot of money and then murdered when he refused to be intimidated."

The Griffin snorted. "You have a good imagination."

"Where were you three nights ago?"

"Sleeping at home, of course. I went to bed early. I thought you'd arrested me for a business crime, Inspector? Have you evidence to support a more serious crime?"

The man was right. Basil had absolutely no proof of The Griffin's involvement in Roland Wilcox's murder. As yet, no physical evidence had been produced and no witnesses. Basil had to stick to questioning him about the long firm frauds for now. He had only hinted at the murder charge to see if it would rattle The Griffin, which it had not.

"Rest assured, we shall get to Roland Wilcox's murder in good time," Basil said and then took a long, relaxed drag on his cigarette. "What I would like to know is why you're not fighting in France, rather than cheating honest businessmen out of hard-earned money? You seem fit enough after all."

"I work in a reserved occupation."

"Really? I wasn't aware that racketeering and fraud were reserved occupations."

"Very funny, Inspector. The truth is that I work on a farm."

"I would bet my best hat that you've never milked a cow, gathered eggs, or tilled a field." Basil tapped his cigarette on the edge of a tin ashtray on the table. "You know that conscription evasion will get you into prison even faster than business fraud these days."

"I will give you the farmer's name, and he will swear on a Bible that I am in his employ."

"Yes, I bet he would, if not just to keep his throat from being cut like Roland Wilcox."

The Griffin raised an eyebrow.

"Or thrown off a bridge, like you threatened to do to Percy Aspen."

The prisoner shrugged. "Never heard the name."

"Who do you get to do that kind of work, by the way?" Basil asked. "The killing, I mean. Is it the same group that helped you buy out the businesses and cheat the suppliers, or is it a different bunch of thugs?"

That earned Basil a snide smirk from The Griffin.

"Ah, I see," said Basil. "You like doing it yourself. That's the nasty side you talked about in your letter, eh?" Basil lazily pointed the end of his cigarette at The Griffin. "You also said you were territorial. That's the part that got to some of these businessmen here. So far, none of them have agreed to testify because you told them that you would go after their wives after you'd killed them. You told them you would make them your wives, in a manner of speaking. That's very nasty indeed." Basil shook his head. "It seems you are very territorial."

The Griffin nodded slowly. "Hence, my nickname."

"Which you apparently acquired in Liverpool. You then moved your operations to London because the heat was being turned up on you there by the local authorities."

"So you say."

"Not just me. I have a source who filled me in on some of your earlier activities which involve racketeering, horse-race gambling, and of course, your favourite, long firm schemes. Did I miss anything off that list?"

The Griffin sighed as if he were battling boredom.

"What I want to know, Mr. Sharp, are the names of those who helped you. There is no way you could have done all this yourself. You had to have friends—well, friends wouldn't be the right word. Men like yourself only use people. You don't form friendships, more like uncomfortable associations founded on a purely transactional basis."

Basil paused before continuing, "That's probably why you never married. Although it wouldn't be a stretch to think you have an illegitimate child somewhere."

That was a wild swing, but it earned Basil a response. The Griffin leaned in, his beady eyes latching on to Basil's. "You leave my daughter out of this, you hear?"

"I've no beef with any child of yours."

"Good. Then I have no beef with any wife of yours."

Basil's mind flashed to Emelia and what a man like this or his thugs would do to her. He forced the fear that flashed through his heart to the floor, butting out his cigarette to buy time. His best bet was to ignore the personal threat, leaving the question about how much Sharp knew about his personal life for another time, and get down to the business at hand.

"Mr. Sharp, if you give me the names of the people who helped you, I promise it will go better for you in front of the judge when it comes time for sentencing."

"You keep saying that. Look, if no one will testify against me, and if I am legitimately employed in a reserved occupation, then you've got nothing." The Griffin's eyes flickered with anger. "I'll soon be making you pay for this indignity, Inspector Reed!"

Basil met The Griffin's angry gaze with his own. "You'll find I don't frighten as easily as your fraud victims, Mr. Sharp. Your day in court is close, and I think you'll find I have a great deal more than nothing."

Basil stood, looked down at the package of Craven A, and then pushed them towards The Griffin. "I think you'd better take that cigarette now. In fact, take the whole packet. You'll need them soon to steady your nerves."

30

After leaving Miss Burton, Ginger and Basil motored quickly to the flat where the woman impersonating Miss Chapman had been staying.

"Hopefully, Braxton is still there," Basil said.

However, when they turned onto the street, there was no sign of a police motorcar anywhere. Having been to the flat before, Ginger led the way up the stairwell, which smelled of someone's meal of fried sausages and potatoes.

When she got to the door of the Chapman flat, she found it slightly ajar. "That's not a good sign," she said as she pushed it open.

Nothing had changed inside since the last time Ginger had been there, except for a white envelope on the table. The words *Scotland Yard* were written on it in sharp, left-leaning cursive. Ginger removed the sheet of paper, a short note with the same handwriting, much like the handwriting in Mr. Aspen's threatening letters.

It read simply:

Until we meet again.

The only salutation was a rough sketch of a lion with the head of an eagle.

Basil cursed. "The Griffin."

"How is that possible?" Ginger asked. "The man's in prison. Assuming he's flesh and blood and not a mythical creature that can transform itself, he couldn't have killed Mr. Aspen or written this note."

"He has a henchman," Basil returned. "Possibly a man who was in prison with him and recently released."

"No one like that was at the Savoy," Ginger reminded him.

"However, the henchman could've threatened one of our three suspects into acting on his behalf."

"That doesn't explain the 'Miss Chapman performance'." Ginger paced in a small circle. "If you recall, Mr. Aspen did seem rather confused by her appearance, as if he didn't quite believe it was her."

"People can change a lot in eleven years," Basil said. "Which is probably why he didn't express his doubts at that moment. And we mustn't disregard his poor eyesight. Perhaps the imposter was counting on this liability. If we can find her, we'll also learn who of the three, Miss Burton, Lawrence, or Yardley, worked in tandem to bring about Aspen's death."

Basil took a step towards the door. "I'm going to go back to the Yard and do more digging. There has to be a clue somewhere as to the imposter's identity."

"I'm needed at home," Ginger said. She hated to leave Rosa for more than a couple of hours at a time. "If you learn anything, ring me there. I have work to do for Feathers & Flair waiting for me in my study."

Basil dropped Ginger off at home. "Give Rosa my love," he said. "I'd come in, but this case is pressing."

"I completely understand," Ginger said, giving her husband a quick kiss goodbye. "Once we get to the bottom of this mystery, we can spend plenty of time together as a family. Scout's coming home at the weekend too!"

In that miraculous all-knowing way he had, Pippins greeted Ginger at the front door and relieved her of her coat and hat.

"Good day, madam," he said.

"Good day, Pips!"

"Madam, you have a caller in the sitting room."

Ginger paused. "Who is it, Pips?"

"Lord Davenport-Witt."

How odd.

Boss, hearing his mistress arrive, scampered across the black-and-white tiles to greet her. Ginger bent down to scoop him into her arms. "Bossy, let's go and see what brings Charles our way."

The sitting room was warmed by gentle flames flickering in the fireplace, and though it was daytime, the grey skies outside prevented enough sunlight from coming through the tall windows to sufficiently light the room. The problem was eradicated by the recently installed electric sconce lighting that had replaced the gas light that had been there for decades.

When he saw Ginger enter, Charles rose from his position on the armchair. "Ginger, forgive my calling on you in this manner."

"Of course." Ginger took the armchair opposite Charles as he sat again, and placed Boss on her lap. "Where is Felicia?" she asked.

"Hair appointment. It's better if she's not aware that I'm here, otherwise, well, her questions would be awkward."

Ginger only nodded. She and Charles shared the unfortunate situation of having taken an oath of secrecy after the war. She'd had her share of uncomfortable conversations with Basil in the past.

"I assume you have news regarding Percival Aspen," she said.

"Through my sources, I learned of intelligence

regarding the man known as Mortimer Sharp and the case involving Mr. Aspen."

Ginger waited, somewhat impatiently, for Charles to get to the point.

"Mortimer Sharp had a daughter. Illegitimate and raised by a prostitute in Liverpool. She was nine at the time of Sharp's incarceration."

"That would make her twenty now," Ginger said as she stroked Boss' black fur. "The approximate age of our imposter's 'niece', Vera Chapman."

"With the right make-up, including a fake mole on her cheek and a prosthetic nose to hide her freckles, she could've passed herself off as Aspen's Winifred, intending to gain revenge for testifying at her father's trial."

"A young girl of nine, robbed of her father's love and attention—however much of that Mortimer Sharp was capable of—could become consumed with gaining revenge on the man who took that from her," Ginger said. "Even to create a plan as elaborate as this. First seeking Mr. Aspen out in South America, then writing the letters with the hope of bringing him back to London."

"For what purpose?" Charles posed.

"I think he was going to ask for help and protection," Ginger said. "If he felt Mortimer Sharp had found him in Brazil, he might not have felt safe anywhere."

"How does Miss Burton fit in?"

"I believe she was a bit of good luck. An unplanned but useful ploy to get close to Mr. Aspen," Ginger said. "I am still unclear as to how she killed him. She was seated at the other end of the table and arrived after the pre-dinner champagne. Even though the lights went out, they weren't out long enough for her to work her way to Mr. Aspen, poison him, and return to her chair with no one noticing."

Charles leaned forward, planting his elbows on his knees. "I have a theory about that. The post-mortem indicated that Lucineride was in Aspen's system, isn't that right?"

Ginger nodded. "Yes."

"I propose that Vera Sharp coated her lips with a wax barrier."

"And that the poison was in her lipstick?" Ginger said with astonishment. "Rather risky, don't you think? And she only kissed him briefly on the forehead." Ginger considered how easy it would have been to accidentally ingest the poison and offered another possibility. "It could have been applied to her gloves. She did take a good hold of his cheeks."

"Jolly good hypothesis," Charles agreed. "You can see why I came to you straight away, Ginger. This Vera

Sharp is a very dangerous character. You and Basil must take every precaution."

Ginger agreed. Guiding Boss to the floor, she got to her feet. "I need to ring Basil. Can you wait, or are you needed somewhere?"

Charles was already on his feet, following Ginger to her study. "I can wait."

Ginger dialled the operator from her black rotary telephone and asked to be connected to Basil at Scotland Yard. "It's urgent."

Constable Braxton answered her call instead. "I'm sorry, Mrs. Reed. Chief Inspector Reed has gone out."

"Do you know where he went?" she asked.

"A lady rang for him, said she had information on the Percival Aspen case. He was to meet her at the Savoy."

Ginger's heart dropped to her heels. "Did he mention the name of the lady?"

"Ah, only her first name, madam. He said she was called Vera."

31

*B*asil turned to look at the courtroom's rear oak door for the sixth time and repeatedly glanced at his watch. In the public gallery, Chief Inspector Morris sat beside him and also leaned over to look at Basil's watch.

"He's very late," Morris said gruffly.

Basil didn't need to be reminded. Their star witness was supposed to have arrived over an hour ago, at the start of the trial. The accountant, Percival Aspen, wouldn't be asked to testify until after the break, but his tardiness was worrisome.

Only a few people were present in the public gallery, mostly members of the press. Much to Basil's surprise, this included Cecil Lawrence from a London rag. He'd positioned himself at the far side of the room and had avoided Basil's gaze.

On the judge's bench and dressed in a traditional black robe and white wig presided Judge Bertrand Flitcroft, his glasses perched at the end of his nose as he read the letter Mortimer Sharp had sent to Basil at Scotland Yard. The prosecuting barrister, Mr. James Latimer, was dressed similarly and had received a copy of the letter, which he also read at the prosecution's desk. Mortimer Sharp, dressed in an expensive-looking suit, sat calmly in the dock at the back of the courtroom, a custody officer at his side. The Griffin's expression was his usual confident smugness.

"This letter is inconclusive," Judge Flitcroft said, waving the paper in the air. "It's signed with this little drawing that could be a bird, a badger, or a fox." He stared down at the defence barrister, Mr. Edward Price. "Mr. Price, you've done a good job proving the defendant's colleagues and business associates sometimes refer to him by this strange nickname . . . what is it again?" He looked at his notes. "Yes . . . the Griffin. But it doesn't follow that this letter is, in fact, signed by him."

"Exactly, your honour," Mr. Latimer said, making a show of shaking his head as if the whole thing was a preposterous notion.

The judge looked at the prosecuting barrister. "Next witness, please."

Mr. Price stood. "Yes, your Honour. The defence calls Mr. Jim Cranshaw to give evidence."

A man in his late sixties, dressed in a tweed suit and wearing round wire-framed spectacles, made an effort to stand with the help of a cane. From where Basil was seated, it was easy to see a look of fierce determination in the man's eyes, which peered out from under white, bushy eyebrows.

It had taken some doing, but Basil had finally convinced the elderly textile importer to testify against The Griffin. Jim Cranshaw was one of the business owners who Roland Wilcox had gathered together to talk about their experiences of being the victims of long firm fraud. All those businessmen were useful to the investigation because they had given Basil some good information. None, however, would agree to testify. Until the news of Roland Wilcox's murder came to Jim Cranshaw.

"I'm old enough now that I don't have much to lose anymore," he'd said as he sat beside Basil in Edward Price's office. "My wife has passed away, and my children live in America. I'm all alone here. Deuced if I'm going to let Wilcox's murder go unanswered."

Basil and Edward Price had exchanged looks of satisfaction and then congratulated the man for his courage and integrity.

"You own the company called Cranshaw Textiles,"

Price began after Jim Cranshaw had taken his position, standing in the witness box. "Can you tell us about your dealings with Mortimer Sharp?"

Cranshaw stared at Sharp with a watery-eyed look of contempt. "I met with that scoundrel only once, but it was enough for him to tell me a multitude of lies."

"Like what, Mr. Cranshaw?" Price asked.

"He told me that he was the new buying manager at Hill Clothiers, specialising in men's apparel. Fine company—at least it was. They have shops in several London districts. He told me that the old buying manager had passed away and that he was now doing the purchasing. Anyway, he convinced me to put in a huge order of material for him, because his stores were preparing for a new expansion in Manchester. I authorised that shipment and several more. Then, when payment for the materials came due, he was nowhere to be found. Hill Clothiers' shops were either boarded up or were shoe shops or some other deuced thing."

"And you received no payment for all those goods?"

Cranshaw's fiery gaze landed yet again on The Griffin. "Not a farthing."

"No other questions, Your Honour," Price said, returning to his seat.

Judge Flitcroft addressed the defence. "The witness is yours, Mr. Latimer."

Latimer rose to his feet to approach the box and

began the following exchange: "Mr. Cranshaw, what was the date of your meeting with the defendant?"

"The date? Well, it was October of 1915 . . . or wait, no, it must have been November."

"The exact date please?"

"Oh, I don't know. I'm retired now, you know. That was a while ago."

"Your manager must have that recorded somewhere?"

"Well, I . . . no, I don't think so."

"So, you can't give me a date?"

Jim Cranshaw sat mutely, then said, "The fourteenth of October, or wait . . . no, that was my wife's birthday. It was November, the fourteenth of November!"

Mr. Latimer flipped through a pocket diary. "You met on a Sunday?"

"No, that's not right either. It must have been November the fifteenth. Yes, yes, it was the fifteenth of November."

"I can prove the defendant was visiting friends in Cornwall on that day, Your Honour."

Basil shifted uneasily on the hard bench. Clearly, the defence intended to confuse the elderly man to discredit him.

"Mr. Cranshaw," Latimer continued, "Can you tell

me then, what exact materials were allegedly ordered by the man you say you met with?"

"Materials you make men's clothing with, of course, everything from cotton to wool, corduroy, leather . . ."

"Hill Clothiers never sold anything to do with leather, corduroy, or cotton," Latimer said, turning to the judge. "In fact, they only sold fine business apparel, expensive suits made from gaberdine, wool, velvet, and imported silk. I have every advert the company produced going back two years."

"Is that true, Mr. Cranshaw?" the judge asked.

Cranshaw scowled. "I can't recall the precise materials because there was so much ordered in a short period."

"I see," Latimer said, flashing a look of pity, which he ensured the jury could see. "You say large amounts of material were ordered. Surely, you can remember those amounts. It would have been an unusual number, wouldn't it?"

Basil watched in dismay as the fierce determination in Mr. Cranshaw's eyes faded to a mixture of hesitancy, bewilderment, and annoyance, common for ageing people whose minds weren't as sharp as they once were. In the early stages, these symptoms were sometimes brought on or exacerbated only when under emotional pressure, like in a witness box. Basil was sure the judge noticed it too.

Blast it!

"I . . . *don't remember exactly,*" Mr. Cranshaw said, his confidence diminishing.

"What was Mortimer Sharp wearing when you met with him?"

"A suit, I imagine!"

"Where did you meet?"

"In my office."

"So, your secretary would have a record of it?"

"We didn't keep those kinds of records," Jim Cranshaw said with irritation.

"Can we get the secretary as a witness? Perhaps he'll remember," The defence barrister turned to the prosecutor. "Oh wait, he passed away last year, didn't he?"

Silence descended in the courtroom. Basil cursed under his breath.

Smugly, Latimer said, "No further questions, Your Honour."

During a short recess, Basil and Morris huddled together in a corridor corner. "Bloody hell!" Morris said, his voice reverberating off the high, arched ceilings and the marble-tiled floor.

"Cranshaw's an old man," Basil said with a sigh. "It's not surprising the defence went after his mental weaknesses. Unfortunately, none of the others would *risk it, with families to think of. Hopefully, Aspen will show up. He's our last shot."*

Cecil Lawrence poked his head out of the large oak doors of the trial room. Basil waved him over.

"Mr. Lawrence," Basil said. "Good of you to join us."

"Just getting some air," the small man said, looking apprehensively at Basil and Morris. Today, he was nicely dressed in a crisp white shirt, black tie, waistcoat, and highly polished leather shoes. Basil wondered if the man had to shop for clothes in the boys' section of the department stores to find such a good fit for himself.

"London sent you to cover this?" Basil asked.

The trial announcement hadn't appeared in any of the papers, but it looked like at least a couple of them would carry the story when the trial ended. If the judge ruled in Mortimer Sharp's favour, Basil and the rest of Scotland Yard would receive bad publicity.

Basil had slept little the night before.

"Yes, well, I was not in favour of being here, but my boss insisted," Cecil Lawrence said. He glanced stealthily down the corridor as if, even now, he was worried that his safety was in jeopardy.

"Will you connect him by name to his past deeds in Liverpool in your story?" Basil asked.

"I don't have to explain or defend myself and how I

do my job to you, Inspector," Lawrence said curtly, walking past them towards the facilities.

"If Lawrence had a modicum of courage and integrity, he could help get The Griffin behind bars," Basil said.

"Aspen!"

Morris' grumble alerted Basil to the figure of Percy Aspen, who walked quickly towards them.

"Good God, man," Price bellowed as he joined them. "The nick of time, eh? The judge is ready to resume."

"We expected you a bit earlier, Mr. Aspen," Morris said.

"I'm sorry." Aspen raised his palms. "I can't do it. I just thought I would come along in person during the break to let you know. I just can't do it."

This brought exclamations of frustration from all three men.

"Why on earth not?" Basil said. "We've practically formed a police barricade around you, your home, and your place of employment. How the devil did anyone get through to you?"

"No one got through to me," Aspen said anxiously. "I'm just having second thoughts, that's all."

Morris blustered, "Don't be daft, man!"

"Look, Mr. Aspen," Price said calmly. "I know this

is an uncomfortable situation, but we've gone over this. You'll do fine."

Aspen looked unconvinced. "I know, I . . ."

"Mr. Aspen," Basil began, "that man in the dock has cheated, bilked, and possibly murdered decent men. He has stolen the lifesavings of families, depriving their children of the future they might have had." He gave him a firm look. "And all you have to do is utter a few sentences to stop him in his tracks."

Aspen blinked rapidly as he blew air out of his cheeks. "Inspector . . ."

Basil pressed on. "Do you realise that if you don't do this, he could walk away from here a free man? He would no doubt cheat again, perhaps kill again. Innocent people could die." Basil stared the scared man in the eye. "You would carry that for the rest of your life, Aspen."

Price repeated Basil's assertion, twisting the proverbial knife a little more. "Mortimer Sharp would undoubtedly find out that you came close to testifying. It's inevitable. That would likely put him in the mood to make sure you never consider it again, if you know what I mean. Men like that don't like loose ends. Set him free today, Mr. Aspen, and one day he'll come for you, of that, I am sure."

Morris added his twopenn'orth. "I don't envy the

sore neck you'll have from constantly looking over your shoulder for the rest of your life."

Percival Aspen looked close to weeping.

The oak doors opened, and an announcement was made that the proceedings were about to continue.

Percy Aspen's mouth came together in a hard line, and his shoulders squared. "Very well, I'll do it."

Aspen stood in the witness box and produced a veritable fountain of damning information against The Griffin: how he was asked to illegally change the financial records of several newly bought businesses, who had asked him to do it, how he had been threatened, and how, after several weeks, he had refused to do it anymore and subsequently fled the city for a time. Every detail was meticulously described and backed up by official written records he had given to the prosecution.

It was an abrupt change of direction for the trial.

Latimer tried his best to attack Aspen's character and motive, but even the most casual observer would have noticed that the attack was flat and carried no merit. Written statements gathered by the prosecution from Aspen's former employers, dating back years, told of a man with impeccable acumen and astuteness on the job.

As Percy Aspen shakily stepped down from the witness box, Mortimer Sharp sprang up in the dock and shouted, "I'll get you for this, you little weasel! You'll pay, do you hear me? Put that in your books. you little—!"

Two courtroom guards quickly descended upon Sharp. The sudden sound of the judge's gavel coming down filled the courtroom.

Basil rushed over to the frightened accountant as he stood shaking beside the witness box..

"I feel that I must flee the country," Aspen said.

"It might not be a bad idea," Basil concurred. "For a time."

32

*S*he'd invited him back to the Savoy.

The woman he now knew to be Vera Sharp was many things: cheeky, daring, conniving, and when she wanted to be, beautiful.

Basil blinked back his confusion and surprise when he saw her seated at a table, white cloth with a small bunch of flowers in a vase in the centre, at the Savoy tearoom. He didn't spot her at first, looking instead for a dowdy version of her Winifred Chapman persona. When the sophisticated young lady with bobbed and wavy hair bleached a platinum blonde waved gloved fingers in his direction, it was all he could do to keep from gasping.

A master of disguise.

Basil removed his trilby, then walked towards her

with all the confidence his position and authority at the Yard gave him.

"I'm so glad you could make room for me in your diary, Inspector Reed," Miss Sharp said with a purr through lips thick with bright red lipstick. "I so hoped we could meet before I leave town."

Basil settled in his seat and chuckled. "What makes you think you're leaving town, Miss Sharp?"

She tilted her head and stared over thick dark lashes, a move Basil was certain had made the knees of many men turn to water.

She smiled seductively. "I tend to get what I want."

After ordering a pot of tea, a waiter came by pushing a trolley with a selection of cakes. Basil kept his eye on Vera Sharp, his mind trying to work out her next move. Surely, she must know that he wouldn't let her leave without arresting her.

What was the daughter of Mortimer Sharp playing at?

The waiter asked, "A slice of cake for you today?"

"No, thank you," Basil said.

Miss Sharp said, "Yes, please." Then, with a glint in her eye added, "Make it two."

"I can assure you, I'll not be indulging in the second cake, Miss Sharp." With an eagle eye, Basil had ensured that Vera Sharp didn't have an opportunity to contaminate his teacup as the waiter poured a fresh round of tea. He didn't doubt her sleight of hand abilities, so he immediately moved his teacup and saucer to his far right and out of her reach.

She noticed. "You don't have to worry, Inspector. I have no intention of killing you by poisoning your tea."

"But you do have the intention of killing me?"

She captured a portion of lemon cake on her fork. "Oh, don't put words into my mouth, Inspector." She opened her mouth and landed the cake in it, as if in slow motion, making the normal daily practice of eating appear obscene.

Basil wasn't going to fall for her antics. "Miss Sharp. Did you want to confess?"

Vera Sharp swallowed her cake then sipped her tea. "Confess to what?"

"To the murder of Percival Aspen."

"Oh, that bounder. My father's in prison because of him." She paused, locking her daring gaze on Basil. "But, of course, you know that."

"That answers the why of the murder," Basil said. "Revenge. But please, enlighten me as to the how."

"Well, I tracked him down in Brazil. He thought he was big stuff now that he had money and could finance those exotic expeditions in the Amazon jungle. The press got a whiff of the news and wrote about it. It was only a matter of time before something hit the London rags. He might've tried to prevent it, but eventually, a newshound printed his name."

"And that's when you started writing him threatening letters."

Vera Sharp laughed. "I wanted to make him squirm. I didn't think I could actually do more than that at first." She narrowed her eyes, her emotion turning venomous. "That man took my father from me when I was nine years old. Because of that, I was brought up in a brothel with my whore of a mother."

She pierced Basil with a look. "I'm sure you can imagine what that's meant for me over the years?"

Basil sympathised with Vera Sharp's tragic upbringing and wouldn't wish that on any child, but he doubted that Mortimer Sharp would ever have taken Vera away from her mother.

"Many young ladies have suffered your unfortunate fate, Miss Sharp, but most don't become murderers."

Vera Sharp released a cackling laugh. "I'm not like most, Inspector. Now, back to my story. I lost my mind knowing that Percy Aspen was living the life of Riley whilst I was forced to work the streets. I managed to *acquire* enough money to buy a steamship ticket and went after him myself."

Basil didn't bother asking what she meant by "acquiring" money but wouldn't doubt it included theft amongst other nefarious things.

"I almost missed him. I arrived the day before he planned to leave. Imagine how I laughed when I learned that my letters had driven him to return to London. And he thought you lot could keep him safe."

"How did you learn he'd returned because of your letters."

"That simpleton Helen told me. He confessed it to her one night after she'd seduced him." Before Basil could ask, she spat out, "I could never pretend to fall in love with my target, especially him. No, Helen Burton served my purposes. He bared his heart to her, and she, with misguided feelings of superiority, quite willingly gossiped about it to me."

"And yet, you never killed him then."

"I didn't have an opportunity. He kept with his first-class crowd the whole time, and unfortunately, never stood about the rail in such a way that I could push him overboard without being seen. I realised that I had to work on my execution. After a bit of research, I came up with a rather brilliant plan."

Basil leaned in, eager to get to the meat of things. "Tell me about the night at the Savoy."

Vera Sharp nodded with a look of self-satisfaction. "I'd learned through Helen—she still knew me as Mary

Jones—of Percy Aspen's dinner party plan. As obsessed as I was with his life, I, of course, knew about the woman Winifred Chapman and how he left her high and dry to save his own skin."

"That was a bit of a risk, was it not?" Basil said. "Since the real Winifred Chapman had died five years earlier."

"It was, but news doesn't travel around the globe very fast, and Percy Aspen seemed to be the kind of man who wanted to forget his past. If he had learned of her death, I suppose I would have looked like an idiot, but I gambled that he wouldn't have the backbone to challenge me in time."

"In time?"

"Certainly, you must know that I never meant to stay long."

"How did you know about the cat superstition?"

"Oh, that? That was just a lucky coincidence." She chuckled. "Or unlucky if you were Mr. Aspen."

"And the lights? You must've been the author of the note asking the head waiter to participate in a prank for a fee."

"That was meant to be a decoy. I wanted everyone to be suspected." She smiled slyly. "And it worked. For a while, anyway."

"So, how did you do it? You were seated too far

away to reach across the table without knocking things about."

Vera Sharp removed a tube of lipstick from her clutch handbag and, using a small mirror, carefully applied it. Basil understood from Ginger that such a move was considered tacky and that ladies of worth would excuse themselves to use the facilities.

But Vera Sharp could hardly be considered a lady of worth.

Dropping the tube of lipstick and the mirror into the opened mouth of her handbag, she carefully slipped on a pair of white gloves, then asked coyly. "Do you *really* want to know, Inspector?"

Basil nodded.

After glancing about the busy tearoom, Vera Sharp invited Basil closer with a crook of her finger. "I'll whisper it in your ear."

Before Basil could protest, his prime suspect grabbed his cheeks with both palms of her gloved hands and kissed him on the forehead.

Shooting to his feet, he protested. "Miss Sharp!"

With a glint of performance glory in her eyes, Vera shouted, "How dare you!" Then she slapped him on the cheek.

Stunned, Basil tried to reach for her wrist before she could make another slapping attempt but found his reflexes had dulled. His fist went to his cheek, which felt strangely numb.

Vaguely aware that the whole tearoom was watching, Basil lowered himself into his chair. "How?"

Vera wiggled her fingers.

"The poison's on your gloves?"

With a look of self-importance, Miss Sharp carefully removed the gloves, turning them inside out, and dropped them into her handbag.

Basil's blood curdled with the sudden knowledge that he'd been duped. He reached for his cloth napkin, desperate to wipe the offending substance from his face, but Vera Sharp had snatched it away. "It normally takes fifteen to twenty minutes to kick in," she said. "But the more you thrash about, the faster it will work."

Basil tried to call out for help, but already his tongue was thickening.

Vera blew Basil a kiss. "Goodbye, Inspector."

Finding it hard to breathe, Basil worked at his tie, his fingers feeling thick and useless.

"Help!" His cry was muffled but loud enough to attract the attention of neighbouring tables.

"Is he having a heart attack?" someone said, then louder, "Help, this man is having a heart attack!"

"Basil!"

Ginger. She looked blurry, ethereal, like an angel come to take him to heaven. How had she found him?

Ginger's voice penetrated a thickening layer of slipping consciousness. "Basil, stay with us. Charles and I are here. You're going to be all right."

"Basil? Basil?"

Then darkness.

33

*B*asil walked briskly up the short walkway to Percy Aspen's residence in Farringdon. First, he'd gone to the offices of Smythe and Biggins accountancy firm in central London, where the receptionist informed him that Aspen had abruptly quit his job. She'd given Aspen's address to Basil, and he hurriedly left to track him down.

As Basil rapped on the brass door knocker of the end-of-terrace house, he could hear someone moving about inside. A moment later, Percival Aspen opened the door. He barely glanced at Basil before waving him in. Basil stood in the hall and removed his hat. The flat was kept clean and well organised, what one would expect in the home of an accountant.

"I was just at your place of employment," Basil

called to the retreating form of Percy Aspen. "I just wanted to check up on you. They told me you'd quit."

Aspen nodded. "I told you I needed to leave the country, and I'm leaving. I sent the security man home that you had set up outside my door, too. You just missed him." Standing next to a trunk and two suitcases, he slipped into a Burberry. "You'll have to forgive me, Inspector, for keeping this short. I have a ship to catch."

"Very well. Might I enquire as to where you're sailing?"

"I have a friend in South Africa involved with diamond mining. He has invited me to come in as a partner."

"I understand your urgency, Aspen. Is there anything I can do for you?"

"There is a rather unpleasant errand I've left to last." Plopping his hat on his head, he glanced at Basil sheepishly. "If you'd take it on, I'd be much obliged."

Hesitantly, Basil asked, "What's the task?"

"I've been seeing a young woman for a few months. It's not serious . . . but I believe she had hopes. We had no official understanding, and with my uncertain future, it would be best to just make a clean break of it."

Basil held in the grimace he felt threatening his expression. There was nothing he loathed more than getting involved with matters of the heart, but he owed Aspen something for his trouble.

He sighed, then asked, "What's her name?"

"Winifred Chapman. She works at the London library."

"All right, Aspen, I'll see to Miss Chapman. I do want to thank you on behalf of the Crown, Scotland Yard, and the good people of this city. You've done a good and courageous thing."

Aspen held out his hand. "Goodbye, Inspector."

Amongst other things, like paperwork and filing, Basil fulfilled his promise to Percy Aspen, stopping at the London Library on the way home, but Miss Chapman wasn't there. Basil, rather sheepishly, left her a note informing her of Aspen's regretful departure. It saved Basil a return trip and what would most certainly be an uncomfortable encounter with an emotional female.

By the time he got home, he was ready to put all the unpleasantness behind him and have a nice, relaxing dinner with his wife.

However, upon entering his home, he found it strangely quiet. Emelia often played classical music on the Victrola that Basil had bought as a gift last Christmas, but today, the machine sat idle in the living room, its oak cover uncharacteristically left closed. Basil hadn't seen that cover closed in months.

"Emelia," Basil called with rising unease. It wasn't the first time he'd come home to an empty house, and

Emelia gone for days or weeks at a time. He ran into the kitchen and then to the foot of the stairs, calling, "Emelia, are you there? I know it's the cook's day off, but we can go to a restaurant for dinner."

Basil's chest tightened as he raced up the stairs, dashing into the master bedroom. There it was, on the bed. Another white envelope. Numbly, he retrieved the note and read the words he'd heard before:

Dearest Basil,

I'm truly sorry, but I just can't do it anymore . . .

34

*G*inger retrieved the vial from her handbag as Charles, quick on his feet, caught Basil as he fell. She'd had the foresight to have one delivered to Hartigan House.

"Basil, love?" Ginger said as she administered the antidote. "I'm here. You'll be fine." She forced herself to keep her voice low and calm. Already a crowd had gathered.

"Someone ring for an ambulance," Charles shouted.

Through laboured breath, Basil's lips twitched, and his eyelids fluttered.

"Basil, love? There, there." Ginger offered him water. "Remember, Dr. Gupta said to drink a lot of water." She lifted his head. "You must try."

At first, much of the water ran down Basil's chin,

and Ginger mopped it up with her handkerchief. "Try again, love."

To her relief, Basil swallowed, and though he wasn't sitting up on his own, he leaned against Ginger, who'd tucked a chair in close beside him.

"That's a good fellow," Charles said, cheering Basil on. "You'll be fit as a fiddle soon."

Ginger gave Charles an appreciative glance. Her husband was far from being fit, and she expected he'd be spending a few days in the hospital for good measure.

Basil blinked as awareness returned. "V-vera?"

"Don't worry about her, love," Ginger said. "She can't get far."

Charles had used his pull as a Lord, and other clandestine means, to ensure that no one with the name of Vera Sharp or Vera Chapman or any lady resembling Vera would leave the country. It was small comfort as Vera Sharp had proven to be a master of disguise. Ginger could only hope she'd stay around as her father was still in prison, even if just for a short while longer, as he had been the impetus for her criminal activity to begin with.

Bells and brass horns announced the ambulance. The police, getting word it was Basil who was down, arrived simultaneously. Ginger gave them Vera Sharp's description.

"Be careful, gentlemen," she said. "This woman is cunning, conniving, and manipulative."

"In a word," Charles added, "dangerous."

Ginger was thankful the constables held the nosy parkers back as Basil was put on the stretcher. Holding his hand, Ginger said, "You're going to be fine, love. I'll be right behind the ambulance." In fact, she intended to beat the ambulance there!

Basil held her gaze. "You saved my life. Again."

It was true. And the weight of knowing how close she'd just come to losing him made her heart seize. "We save each other when necessary," she said, her voice catching. "Don't we, love?"

35

*I*t'd been a week since Ginger had brought Basil home from hospital. He was recovering steadily, and the doctors had assured that in time, he would experience a full recovery. At present, the two of them were enjoying a glass of brandy in the sitting room and discussing this sad truth: Not all cases get solved. And not all criminals are caught.

"Britain isn't so large that one woman can hide from the law forever," Ginger said.

"If she's still here."

Ginger didn't want to say it aloud, but an intelligent and skilled woman like Vera Sharp could be anywhere. She'd been the reason Percy Aspen wanted help, at least that was what they presumed, as he hadn't had the chance to fully reveal it that night.

He'd wanted to find out the author of the threatening letters and solicit protection.

"Mortimer Sharp is up for parole soon," Basil added.

Boss climbed onto Ginger's lap, and she embraced the canine comfort.

"Do you think he'll get it?"

"He's been a model prisoner," Basil said with a sigh. "I've no doubt he's been the puppet strings behind his daughter and probably others, but there's no evidence to prove it."

The thought of both the father and daughter on the loose with Basil in their sights gave Ginger the chills. She snuggled into her husband's side, comforted by his presence and by the warmth of the hot coals burning in the fireplace. The house was quiet and at peace with Rosa tucked in bed, Scout at Kingswell, and the staff finished working for the day.

At least the house had been quiet!

The doorbell clanged, and moments later, Louisa's tortured voice echoed through the entrance hall. "How dare he do this to me? The humiliation! Oh, Mama, I'm such a fool."

Unfortunately for Cornelius, Basil had followed up on his story that he'd simply offended Percy Aspen as he led an expedition in Peru, and it had come to light that morning that Cornelius had, in fact, made off with a prized artefact. Mr. Aspen had suspected the theft but couldn't provide proof. Cornelius would've been their prime suspect had Ginger and Basil learned of his crime earlier. As it was, the man had run off, perhaps with misplaced fear. He would be captured and arrested even though the British police had no authority over him in this matter. Or he had quite likely realised Louisa's fortune was now out of his reach.

Louisa's wails swung between heartbroken sobs and outraged indignation.

Sally's no-nonsense voice followed. "You're not a fool, Louisa. You're gullible. Next time, you'll be more careful."

Sobbing, Louisa floated along the tile floors and Sally's words bobbed above it. "Now, now, dear. Time to turn off the waterworks. You have the advantage of telling the story your way. You broke off the engagement before finding out he was a thief. You just sensed something was off. You are the strong and smart one."

"You're right, Mama," Louisa said. After a few moments' pause, her voice changed. "He's not good enough for me. Never was."

Ginger listened to the two Hartigan ladies with a sense of longing. Her own mother had passed away when she was a baby, and she was eight when her father had married Sally. Sally hadn't embraced her as a daughter the way Ginger had embraced Scout as a son, and it hurt a little to hear this mother and daughter interaction between her stepmother and her half-sister.

Turning her focus back to Basil, she said, "A letter came from Scout. He's still very unhappy at the academy, and I'm afraid he's ready to play up."

"We'll spend a lot of time with him when he's home," Basil said. "Hopefully, I'll be ready to play tennis and cricket with him by then."

Ginger shifted to face him. "He's been in touch with Marvin."

"I suppose that's natural," Basil said. "With them being cousins."

"Scout says Marvin has joined the circus."

Basil's forehead buckled. "What happened to the Navy?"

"I made a few calls to find out," Ginger said. She'd pulled strings a couple of years earlier to keep Marvin out of prison in exchange for a service agreement with the Navy. "Sadly, Marvin was dishonourably discharged, due to fighting. Mostly with other sailors, but one brawl led to his fist connecting with the jaw of a senior officer. He was let go immediately without an extra farthing."

"So, the circus was his next bed and meal," Basil said.

"It looks that way." Ginger scratched Boss behind the ear, adding, "I hope he'll be all right there."

"I'm sure he'll be fine, love," Basil said. "Now, let us go to bed. Rosa will wake us up early enough, and we can worry about everything we want to worry about then."

BASIL FOLLOWED his wife up the stairs—now empty of the Hartigan ladies and their dramatic overtures—secure in knowing that the doors and windows were locked, and the police officer he had made previous arrangements for was on watch. He hadn't brought the fact up with Ginger as he hadn't wanted to cause her concern needlessly, but Basil was very uneasy.

He patted the letter in his pocket that'd come to him by messenger that afternoon. Ginger had been busy with the baby, so she wasn't privy to its arrival or its contents.

The words, written in a sharp left-leaning slant, burned on his mind.

Dear Chief Inspector Reed,
*   You haven't seen the last of me.*
*   Vera*

If you enjoyed reading *Murder at the Savoy* please help others enjoy it too.

Recommend it: Help others find the book by recommending it to friends, readers' groups, discussion boards and by **suggesting it to your local library.**

Review it: Please tell other readers why you liked this book by reviewing it on Amazon or Goodreads.

* No spoilers please *

Don't miss the next Ginger Gold mystery~
Murder at the Circus

Murder's a spectacle!

When Ginger Reed ∼ aka Lady Gold ∼ and Basil Reed's son Scout runs away to join the circus, it's not all fun and games. As a disgruntled teen unhappy at boarding school, Scout intends to work with his cousin Marvin, newly (and dishonourably) discharged from the navy, as an animal caretaker.

The big top event pleases the crowds, but when a performer dies under suspicious circumstances, Scout finds himself in real, three ring trouble.

Buy on AMAZON or read Free with Kindle Unlimited!

NOTE FROM THE AUTHOR

THE FAMOUS SAVOY HOTEL

Built in 1889, the Savoy was the first deluxe hotel in London, a real statement of luxury and opulence for its time! In those early days, it was a thing of wonder that the entire building was lit with electric light, powered by electric lifts - and even had the option for both hot and cold water (Can you believe it?) In fact, the hotel became known for its inventiveness and innovations, along with exquisitely lavish rooms and the most **dramatic decor** - fit for royalty!

The most famous and aristocratic people in England couldn't resist a visit - and it's easy to see why.

Air Conditioning was one of the hotel's innovations, and by the late 1920s and mid 30s, most of the hotel was installed with the luxury of cool air!

Kaspar the famous Savoy Cat

Kaspar, the famous Savoy black cat, was carved in 1927 by the designer Basil Ionides.

Today, you will see Kaspar honoured through reproduced statues on the restaurant tables of the Savoy.

Why? Because Kaspar is thought to have brought **good luck** to the hotel.

Story: Woolf Joel, a prominent businessman, held a **goodbye dinner party** with his friends and business acquaintances in 1898, as he was going to leave to Southampton the next morning.

The total people at the dinner party were **13**. It was supposed to be 14, but one of Joel's guests cancelled last minute.

As Joel was getting ready to leave, one guest reminded him of the old superstition that if 13 dined together, the first to leave the table would be destined to die first!

And guess what happened? Only weeks later, Joel was shot dead!

This was not good news for the Savoy and its more superstitious guests. Going forward, no matter what, a 14th guest would need to be present at dinner gatherings of 13.

But, wouldn't it be awkward if that extra guest were a waiter or someone no one knew? The solution: Savoy the cat. A perfect 14th guest, sure to cause no disruptions to the gatherings.

ABOUT LUCINERIDE

Invented "science" is a common ploy in all kinds of fictitious works including books, film and television.

In Murder at the Savoy, the drug *Lucineride* is a creation of the author's imagination.

ACKNOWLEDGMENTS

A big shout out to my husband, Norm Strauss, who joined writing forces with me a while ago to help with the Lady Gold Investigations short story series and the Rosa Reed Mystery series.

Until now, I've penned all of the Ginger Gold Mystery series novels on my own, but Norm jumped in on this one as a ghost writer to draft the Basil Reed back story. It's gone so well, I'm sure he'll be helping out with more Ginger books!

GINGER GOLD'S JOURNAL

Sign up for Lee's readers list and gain access to **Ginger Gold's private Journal.** Find out about Ginger's Life before the SS *Rosa* and how she became the woman she has. This is a fluid document that will cover her romance with her late husband Daniel, her time serving in the British secret service during World War One, and beyond. Includes a recipe for Dark Dutch Chocolate Cake!

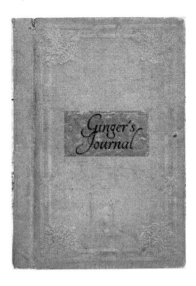

It begins: **July 31, 1912**

How fabulous that I found this Journal today, hidden in the bottom of my wardrobe. Good old Pippins, our English butler in London, gave it to me as a parting gift when Father whisked me away on our American adventure so he could marry Sally. Pips said it was for me to record my new adventures. I'm ashamed I never even penned one word before today. I think I was just too sad.

This old leather-bound journal takes me back to that emotional time. I had shed enough tears to fill the ocean and I remember telling Father dramatically that I was certain to cause flooding to match God's. At eight years old I was well-trained in my biblical studies, though, in retro-spect, I would say that I had probably bordered on heresy with my little tantrum.

The first week of my "adventure" was spent with a tummy ache and a number of embarrassing sessions that involved a bucket and Father holding back my long hair so I wouldn't soil it with vomit.

I certainly felt that I was being punished for some reason. Hartigan House—though large and sometimes lonely—was my home and Pips was my good friend. He often helped me to pass the time with games of I Spy and Xs and Os.

"Very good, Little Miss," he'd say with a twinkle in his blue eyes when I won, which I did often. I suspect now that our good butler wasn't beyond letting me win even when unmerited.

Father had got it into his silly head that I needed a mother, but I think the truth was he wanted a wife. Sally, a woman half my father's age, turned out to be a sufficient wife in the end, but I could never claim her as a mother.

Well, Pips, I'm sure you'd be happy to

know that things turned out all right here in America.

SUBSCRIBE to read more!

.

ABOUT THE AUTHOR

Lee Strauss is a USA TODAY bestselling author of The Ginger Gold Mysteries series, The Higgins & Hawke Mystery series, The Rosa Reed Mystery series (cozy historical mysteries), and others with over a million books read. She has titles published in German, Spanish and French, and a growing audio library.

When Lee's not writing or reading she likes to cycle, hike, and stare at the ocean. She loves to drink caffè lattes and red wines in exotic places, and eat dark chocolate anywhere.

For more info on books by Lee Strauss and her social media links, visit leestraussbooks.com. To make sure you don't miss the next new release, be sure to sign up for her readers' list!

Discuss the books, ask questions, share your opinions. Fun giveaways! Join the Lee Strauss Readers' Group on Facebook for more info.

Love the fashions of the 1920s? Check out Ginger Gold's Pinterest Board!

Did you know you can follow your favourite authors on Bookbub? If you subscribe to Bookbub — (and if you don't, why don't you? - They'll send you daily emails alerting you to sales and new releases on just the kind of books you like to read!) — follow me to make sure you don't miss the next Ginger Gold Mystery!

www.leestraussbooks.com
leestraussbooks@gmail.com

MORE FROM LEE STRAUSS

On AMAZON

GINGER GOLD MYSTERY SERIES (cozy 1920s historical)

Cozy. Charming. Filled with Bright Young Things. This Jazz Age murder mystery will entertain and delight you with its 1920s flair and pizzazz!

Murder on the SS Rosa

Murder at Hartigan House

Murder at Bray Manor

Murder at Feathers & Flair

Murder at the Mortuary

Murder at Kensington Gardens

Murder at St. George's Church

The Wedding of Ginger & Basil

Murder Aboard the Flying Scotsman

Murder at the Boat Club

Murder on Eaton Square

Murder by Plum Pudding

Murder on Fleet Street

Murder at Brighton Beach

Murder in Hyde Park

Murder at the Royal Albert Hall

Murder in Belgravia

Murder on Mallowan Court

Murder at the Savoy

Murder at the Circus

LADY GOLD INVESTIGATES (Ginger Gold companion short stories)

Volume 1

Volume 2

Volume 3

Volume 4

HIGGINS & HAWKE MYSTERY SERIES (cozy 1930s historical)

The 1930s meets Rizzoli & Isles in this friendship depression era cozy mystery series.

Death at the Tavern

Death on the Tower

Death on Hanover

Death by Dancing

THE ROSA REED MYSTERIES

(1950s cozy historical)

Murder at High Tide

Murder on the Boardwalk

Murder at the Bomb Shelter

Murder on Location

Murder and Rock 'n Roll

Murder at the Races

Murder at the Dude Ranch

Murder in London

Murder at the Fiesta

Murder at the Weddings

A NURSERY RHYME MYSTERY
SERIES (mystery/sci fi)

Marlow finds himself teamed up with intelligent and savvy Sage Farrell, a girl so far out of his league he feels blinded in her presence - literally - damned glasses! Together they work to find the identity of @gingerbreadman. Can they stop the killer before he strikes again?

Gingerbread Man

Life Is but a Dream

Hickory Dickory Dock

Twinkle Little Star

THE PERCEPTION TRILOGY (YA dystopian mystery)

Zoe Vanderveen is a GAP—a genetically altered person. She lives in the security of a walled city on prime water-front property along side other equally beautiful people with extended life spans. Her brother Liam is missing. Noah Brody, a boy on the outside, is the only one who can help ～ but can she trust him?

Perception

Volition

Contrition

LIGHT & LOVE (sweet romance)

Set in the dazzling charm of Europe, follow Katja, Gabriella, Eva, Anna and Belle as they find strength, hope and love.

Sing me a Love Song

Your Love is Sweet

In Light of Us

Lying in Starlight

PLAYING WITH MATCHES (WW2

history/romance)

A sobering but hopeful journey about how one young German boy copes with the war and propaganda. Based on true events.

A Piece of Blue String (companion short story)

THE CLOCKWISE COLLECTION (YA time travel romance)

Casey Donovan has issues: hair, height and uncontrollable trips to the 19th century! And now this ∼ she's accidentally taken Nate Mackenzie, the cutest boy in the school, back in time. Awkward.

Clockwise

Clockwiser

Like Clockwork

Counter Clockwise

Clockwork Crazy

Clocked (companion novella)

Standalones

Seaweed

Love, Tink

27758226R00141